Christmas in Manhattan

All the drama of the ER, all the magic of Christmas!

A festive welcome to Manhattan Mercy ER—a stone's throw from Central Park in the heart of New York City. Its reputation for top-notch health care is eclipsed only by the reputation of the illustrious, wealthy Davenport family and the other dedicated staff who work there!

With snow about to blanket New York over Christmas, ER chief Charles Davenport makes sure his team is ready for the drama and the challenge…but when it comes to love, a storm is coming the likes of which they've never seen before!

Available now:

Sleigh Ride with the Single Dad by Alison Roberts

A Firefighter in Her Stocking by Janice Lynn

The Spanish Duke's Holiday Proposal by Robin Gianna

Aristocratic paramedic Mateo Alves needs a temporary fiancée, but will he be able to let Dr. Miranda Davenport go when the holiday is over?

The Rescue Doc's Christmas Miracle by Amalie Berlin

Risk-taking air ambulance paramedic Penny Davenport has a secret to tell her partner, the cautious, wary Dr. Gabriel Jackson—she's pregnant with his child!

Christmas .... sle

Navy Doc o..ttan

Dear Reader,

It's always a pleasure to get to work with other authors on a continuity like this one! The Davenport siblings are certainly interesting, with challenging dynamics and a few family struggles, but they all eventually get their happily-ever-afters. :)

I love that the editors set my story mostly in Spain. I enjoy researching interesting places, and Spain was no exception. One thing that surprised me is that there really are a large number of dukedoms in the country!

This is the first book I've written with the fake-engagement trope, which was fun. ER doctor Miranda Davenport agrees to help Mateo with the ruse, partly because her life history has made her a people-pleaser, and because she knows what it's like to feel like you may not live up to your family's expectations. Mateo Alves, EMT and member of the Spanish nobility, thinks Miranda is just the woman to stand up to his parents. They're pushing him to move back home, marry and take over running the family estate, but he wants to keep his life in New York City. Then he finds out that Miranda may be a great doctor, but her toughness and confidence are a veneer she puts on to cover her vulnerabilities, and he's placed her in a situation that reminds her of past pain in her life.

Mateo and Miranda help each other reconcile their pasts and see that things they've always believed about their roles in their families aren't entirely true. They've both held close a deep conviction that they've never measured up, but by seeing each other carrying these false beliefs, they learn to let go of their own.

xoxo

Robin

THE SPANISH DUKE'S HOLIDAY PROPOSAL

———

ROBIN GIANNA

HARLEQUIN® MEDICAL ROMANCE™

Recycling programs for this product may not exist in your area.

Special thanks and acknowledgment are given to Robin Gianna for her contribution to the Christmas in Manhattan series.

ISBN-13: 978-0-373-21562-1

The Spanish Duke's Holiday Proposal

First North American Publication 2017

Copyright © 2017 by Harlequin Books S.A.

This edition published by arrangement with Harlequin Books S.A.

For questions and comments about the quality of this book, please contact us at CustomerService@Harlequin.com.

Printed in U.S.A.

Books by Robin Gianna

Harlequin Medical Romance

Royal Spring Babies
Baby Surprise for the Doctor Prince

The Hollywood Hills Clinic
The Prince and the Midwife

Midwives On-Call at Christmas
Her Christmas Baby Bump

Flirting with Dr. Off-Limits
It Happened in Paris…
Her Greek Doctor's Proposal
Reunited with His Runaway Bride

Visit the Author Profile page
at Harlequin.com for more titles.

I'd like to dedicate this book to wonderful fellow medical author Amalie Berlin, who helped me brainstorm parts of this story and was always there when I needed to wail about struggles I had pulling it together. Thanks for always being there, Amalie!
xoxo

A big thanks to Dr. Meta Carroll for helping me with the medical scenes in this book, per usual! Meta, you are the best! xoxo

Praise for
Robin Gianna

"Robin Gianna writes stories that will draw you in with their sensuality and emotion and this one was a beauty.... I loved this story from start to finish."

—*Goodreads* on
The Prince and the Midwife

CHAPTER ONE

FOR HEAVEN'S SAKE, can't you go any faster?

Since it was obvious the massive traffic jam made that impossible, Miranda Davenport bit her lip to keep from exclaiming exactly that. Her cab driver seemed as frustrated as she was, not being able to move more than a few feet at a time as the minutes ticked by, and no amount of impatience by either one of them was going to help her get to the hospital sooner. Even from several blocks away, the blue and red strobe-like flashes from multiple emergency vehicles covered the street, jammed so heavily with cars that could only inch along every five minutes or so.

"Subway tunnel collapse must be bad. Hope it isn't a terrorist attack," her cab driver said.

"Yeah. Me, too." The thought of the subway tunnel collapse being done by terrorists made Miranda shiver, but she also knew that sometimes things like that happened from structural decay, and prayed that was the case this time.

She also prayed there wouldn't be too many casualties, and she clenched her teeth with impatience because it might be critically important for her to get to the hospital ASAP. Excruciatingly long minutes ticked by until she couldn't stand sitting there any longer.

"Listen, I think I'm going to get out and walk from here." It was still quite a few blocks to the hospital and her trek home had proved that winter had decided to arrive in New York City with a vengeance. But sitting here barely moving felt torturous when the Manhattan Mercy ER might well be swamped with patients, and they'd called her back, anticipating the worst.

"Hang on a few more minutes, lady. Let me see what I can do."

Like so many of the drivers whose vehicles filled the street, her cabbie honked his horn, and Miranda nearly clamped her hands to her ears at the cacophony. Growing up in Chicago then living in New York City for the past thirteen years meant the sound of car horns usually faded into the background. But after being stuck in the middle of this traffic mess for the past half-hour, it was starting to give her the mother of all headaches. Or maybe her headache was from not enough sleep after the twelve-hour shift she'd just worked in the ER, not expecting a catastrophe to bring her back before she was even home.

The cab managed to move a couple feet before the driver laid on the horn again, and Miranda knew the poor guy was going to be creeping along in this traffic for a long time. "Sorry, but I've got to get to the hospital. Thanks for bringing me this far. Here's extra for your trouble." Never having had that "extra" in her younger life was something she'd never forget, and even after all this time it felt good to be able to share the wealth. She shoved a fold of cash through the window to the front seat, then opened her door to exit right in the middle of the street. Not that dodging between stopped cars to the sidewalk brought any risk to life and limb at that moment.

The frigid air sneaking down her neck felt practically sub-zero, and she grabbed her coat collar, ducked her head down against the wind, and hurried toward the hospital. Good thing she had on the comfortable shoes she always wore to work, and her strides ate up the pavement fairly quickly until she came to the dust particles filling the air. Then she stared in shock at the yawning hole where the pavement had collapsed in the street, the subway tracks clearly visible below. Her heart tripped into double-time as she watched numerous firefighters and paramedics running in and out of the tunnel. Then she yanked herself out of her shocked stupor, moving closer to see if she could assist.

"You have any patients that need help?" she shouted above the chaos. "I'm—"

"You need to move to the other side of the street!" a paramedic yelled back. "It's not safe here."

"I'm an ER doctor, heading to the hospital. Wondering if you need any help here."

"No. We're doing okay. Thanks, but you need to move on."

"Can you tell me how many injured the hospital might be dealing with?"

"Right now, looks like not a lot. The collapse was only in a small area, and not many people were waiting for the train there." He swiped a grimy gloved hand against his forehead. "Unless something else happens, we're hoping for minimal victims. Right now we're focusing on shoring up the tunnel as we search to see who else might be down there."

The air Miranda sucked into her lungs in cautious relief was cold and full of the nasty dust, and she coughed. "Okay. Good luck, and be careful in there."

She pulled her scarf up over her mouth and moved away from the hole to hurry on to the hospital, only to be stopped by police officers who were setting up orange barriers on the sidewalk, insisting she cross over to the other side of the street.

About to argue and tell them her mission, she decided to just do as they asked. There were hardly any pedestrians on the other sidewalk to impede her progress, so she'd be able to walk faster anyway. As she moved across the barricaded street, a sound caught her ears. Something that sounded like someone crying out in the distance, and she stopped, straining to hear. Another faint cry had her heart pumping faster, and she hurried around the barricade in the street to see what was making the sound, abruptly stopping at the sight. Had no one seen this other, small collapse in the pavement? Dust swirled up from a virtual stepping stone of concrete and asphalt, leading down into the darkness.

Had the first responders been so focused on the large collapse that they hadn't discovered it yet? Did they know someone was in there?

She swung around to get the attention of one of the police officers, but they'd moved too far away to hear her. Heart beating in triple-time, she windmilled her arms to get the attention of the firefighters and paramedics, but in the midst of everything going on, nobody noticed a lone woman in a black coat waving at them. It probably didn't help that this hole was a good block away from them now.

Would she lose precious time trying to get help? Her heart jerked at the thought of going down into that tunnel, but she had to do something, right? Whoever was in there might be injured, and surely the paramedics would see this small hole any minute. The question was, would they arrive too late, when she was there right now?

Miranda battled down the fear that rose in her throat as she fished in her purse for the small but bright flashlight she always kept there. Stumbling a little, she picked her way through chunks of asphalt and concrete as quickly as she could, leaning over to place her free hand on the jagged lumps to steady herself as she descended beneath the street. The farther down she went, the harder her heart pounded, finally leaving the light of day completely behind her as she headed into the flat darkness.

She peered through the dark, fighting a slightly panicky feeling of claustrophobia. But she was here now, and she'd never forgive herself for being cowardly and climbing back up when, for all she knew, someone could be dying down here.

"Hello? Anyone there? Are you okay? Do you need help?"

A moan and a shout she couldn't understand came back, which sent adrenaline surging through her blood.

"Hang on! I'm a doctor. I can help if you're hurt."

No answer this time. Moving through the rubble wasn't easy, and she felt beyond frustrated at how hard it was to see through the fine silt filling the tunnel beneath the street, swirling up as occasional small bits of rubble fell from the ceiling. Where were the victims in this mess, and how far inside could they be?

The dust made it hard to breathe, and she coughed, pulling the scarf looped around her neck up to cover her mouth again. Not to mention that she was short of breath from the worry of who might be trapped and if she could help at all. And, oh, yeah, the idea that the whole street might come crashing down was just a tad unnerving. She tripped a few times, until a second beam of light from farther inside the tunnel slashed across her, illuminating the way a little more.

"What the hell are you doing in here? Get out!"

Taken aback by the angry male voice, Miranda stopped in her tracks for a second and didn't answer. Then she gathered her wits and sent her own flashlight toward the voice as she fired back, "I'm here to see if I can help."

"Not if this tunnel collapses on you. Get out of here. Right now. Can't you see it's dangerous down here? There's only one injured person, and

I'm taking care of him. Last thing I need is someone else getting hurt through her own stupidity."

Anger joined the adrenaline heating her veins. Who did this guy think he was? Being told what to do was something she'd hated for years, let alone when it was coming from some hero wannabe. She moved forward again, trying to see through the dust and rubble.

"There's nothing stupid about helping injured people. Where…?" Her flashlight finally landed on two men. One was on the ground, bleeding from his forehead and lying awkwardly on one arm. Even with the lack of light, his pallor told her he was going into shock. The other man was crouched over him, his fingers on the man's neck, apparently trying to get his pulse rate.

"I'm not going to say it again—you need to leave! For all I know, this could be the work of terrorists, with a chemical attack to follow. I've got this guy, and responders will be here any minute."

The thought of a chemical attack sent a shiver down Miranda's back, for both herself and anyone else nearby, but she wasn't going to leave until she knew survivors were taken care of. "Have you seen anyone besides this victim?"

He yanked off his coat, completely ignoring her question. His tone changed so completely when he spoke to the man, its gentle quietness surprised her. "I'm going to move you so I can look at your arm. Try to relax, and don't help, okay?" He slowly rolled the victim to his back with extreme care, wadding his coat up under the man's feet to elevate them, obviously knowing how to treat someone going into shock. Then in one fluid movement he pulled his shirt over his head before ripping it into pieces, pressing one section against the man's forehead. "You hold this against your head wound while I look at your arm."

"My dog," the man said on a moan. "Do you see my dog?"

"Remember? I said I'll look for him after I check you out. And I will, but it's not going to do your dog any favors to have you go into shock, is it?"

The patient nodded in response. Miranda finally reached them and crouched down. "I'm a doctor. I can help."

The bossy man paused to look up at her, his eyes meeting hers in an intense stare before he gave her a quick nod. "All right. Hold his arm steady as I get this off." He pulled a knife from his coat pocket, flipped open the blade, then began quickly and efficiently cutting away the victim's coat sleeve.

"Got it." She briefly flashed her light over the victim's arm, noting the navy-blue sleeve was dark with what was probably blood. She put her flashlight down on the rubble, trying to direct the light toward the man's arm, before she reached to gently but firmly hold it in place as the rest of the sleeve was cut away.

He paused in his cutting to clamp his flashlight between his teeth so he could use both hands and see at the same time he worked, which made Miranda look more carefully at his shadowed and dirty face. His ridiculously handsome face, which she now realized with a start she'd seen before, and that always made her take an involuntary second and third look. A face that belonged to an EMT she'd often seen in the hospital, bringing in patients.

Trying to remember his name, she was filled with a short rush of relief that she wasn't alone in this place, trying to deal with this serious injury before figuring out how to get him to the hospital. That the man working on the patient knew what he was doing, and that they could work together as a team.

The way he was leaning over the patient made it hard to see the man, so she stared at the medic's head instead, tipped downward as he cut away the cloth. She knew his short hair was normally black, but right now gray powder covered both it and his dark brows. More of the silt filtered down onto all three of them, and she swallowed hard, shoving down the fear that skittered down her back again at the thought of being buried alive.

The last of the coat and clothing was cut off, and they were both finally able to see the jaggedly ripped and bleeding flesh of the victim's forearm. While she couldn't see the bone beneath it, there was no doubt this was a compound fracture. Which meant the bleeding had to be stopped and the arm stabilized while trying not to jar the broken pieces in the process.

The medic's eyes met hers, and what she saw there telegraphed loud and clear that he knew as well as she did that if the bones got moved the wrong way, they risked an artery being torn, which would turn a bad situation worse.

He took the flashlight from his teeth and tucked it under his chin. "You still got his arm steady? I'm going to wrap it."

"Yes. You can let go. I have a book in my purse. We can use it as a splint."

He glanced up, his intense eyes meeting hers again. "I have a magazine folded in my coat pocket. I'll use both to stabilize the arm after I get the bleeding stopped, so leave the book, then go."

Ignoring his comment the way he'd ignored hers earlier, she watched him carefully lay a piece of his shirt on top of the bleeding wound, then lift his hand, apparently planning to press down on it.

"Don't do that, you'll dislodge the bones!" she said. "We need to be as careful as possible not to cause further damage. Putting pressure on it isn't a good idea. A tourniquet is a better option to try first."

"I realize that a lowly EMT knows little compared to you, Dr. Davenport," he drawled, emphasizing the word *doctor* as he continued to work quickly, wrapping a strip of torn shirt around either end of the cloth bandage. "But I know a lot more about field medicine than you do and I have the technique down pat."

Surprise that he knew her name was quickly replaced by serious annoyance as his nearly amused tone started to really tick her off. She opened her mouth to retort that an ER doctor was fully trained in all kinds of emergencies. Until that emotion and her words dried up fast as she watched the remarkable efficiency and competency he showed as he tied off a makeshift tourniquet, then held the victim's legs up with one arm as he grabbed his now filthy coat from the ground to pull out a magazine.

All right, she had to admit it, but not to this autocratic male. While she worked hard to be the best doctor she could be, this guy had her beat when it came to this kind of emergency, working without all kinds of medical supplies and the equipment she always had available at her fingertips.

"This is probably going to hurt, so hang on," he said to the patient. "You doing okay?"

"O-Okay," the man said on a gasp that turned into a groan as the medic slowly and carefully straightened his arm. He then curved the magazine beneath the man's elbow.

"Can you—?"

"Yes." She reached to cup her hands underneath to hold it in place as he worked to secure it with strips of his shirt. The patient moaned, and Miranda leaned closer. "I'm sorry, sir. I know it hurts, but the hospital's close by. As soon as we get the wound secured, we'll get you out of here. You're going to be fine, and getting meds to help with the pain really soon."

"Where's that book?" the medic asked, never pausing as he knotted the strips and reached for another.

"Here." With one hand, she slid her bag from her shoulder and reached in to fish out the book. "I'll place it under his wrist when you're done."

A quick nod as he finished up with the magazine, then suddenly lifted his eyes to hers. The quick grin he sent, along with a smile in that brown gaze, took her totally by surprise, and for some ridiculous reason made her heart beat little harder. Apparently helping him had taken her off his list of highly irritating things. For the moment, at least.

"I'm sorry, I should know, but what's your name?" she heard herself ask, suddenly needing to know.

"Mateo Alves. This is John, and his dog, Benny, ran in here after the collapse, which is why John came down here in the first place. He's a fast one for a shorty dog, but I'll find him. And I already know you're Miranda Davenport. I'd say it's nice to meet you, except you shouldn't have come in here to begin with."

"Too bad. There's nothing falling now, so we're probably safe." She knew she sounded a little breathless, which was probably due to the silt in the air and not at all to the fact that she'd fantasized about the über-handsome EMT more than once in the ER. During those times, they'd all been busy treating patients, so there hadn't been time to spend more than a brief moment staring at him, and now wasn't a good time either. Except she found that, for what felt like a long moment of connection between them, she was staring at him anyway.

"Yeah, well, that could change in one second."

She glanced up, gulping at that reality. To cover her worries, she threw out a tart response. "Aren't you going to admit that both of us working on John's arm has been faster than you doing it alone, and better for him?"

"Maybe." Another quick flash of teeth.

"I'm going to put the book under his forearm now."

"Wait. I want to cover the wound better first."

Her rapt attention on his handsome features was interrupted when he frowned and paused in his work on the wrist splint. She looked down and saw that he'd used every scrap of fabric from his torn shirt.

"Give me your scarf."

"Oh. That's a good idea," she said, wishing she'd thought of it. She slipped it from her neck and handed it to him. "And I can cut the bottoms off my pants, too, if we need them."

That flash of grin. "What do you think, John? How often do you have a woman offering to rip her clothes off for you?"

"Not often enough." A weak smile accompanied his words, then disappeared again. "My dog. My Benny. I haven't heard him bark."

"Probably too scared to bark. But I have a surefire way to call dogs—you'll see. Right now, though, we have to get you out of here without jostling your arm any more than necessary. Dr. Davenport?"

"Yes?"

"I'm afraid I'm going to have to take you up on

the offer of your pants. Don't worry, I won't cut any above your knees." That sexy smile again. "But that fabric is a lot better than my jeans to finish securing the splint, since I'm going to use your scarf as a sling to keep it still."

"That makes sense." Of course he'd need a sling, and she thrashed herself that it hadn't occurred to her. Thank God none of her siblings or father could see her. She'd spent the last thirteen years trying to make them proud of her, to earn their respect, and right now she felt totally inept.

She reached for the knife and pushed the point into the knit material. It went in easily, even as she inwardly cringed at the thought of accidentally jabbing herself in her own calf. And being that kind of wimp proved even more that Mateo was absolutely right—he was definitely better at this field medicine stuff than she was, and she vowed to study it again, maybe even go on some runs with the EMTs to refresh her skills.

But not with Mateo Alves. She'd find someone whose sexy face and body wouldn't distract her from her training mission.

"Careful. Don't cut yourself."

"I know how to use a knife."

"Do you cut clothes off yourself on a regular basis? Pretty sure that's harder than cutting a sandwich."

"Funny." She struggled to move the knife down

through the pants leg without gouging herself in the process, and as she did so heard an impatient sound come from Mateo.

"Let me."

"I'm doing fine."

"Yeah? Well, every second is time John isn't at the hospital for pain meds and treatment, and we're all still down here."

"There hasn't been any debris for a while. Right?" She paused in her cutting to look up at the dark tunnel ceiling again, wishing he'd stop pointing out the possibility of impending collapse.

A snorting *humph* was his only response as he tugged the knife from her hand and took over, getting it through the cloth in mere seconds, then hacking it off from around her knee before tearing it into strips. For some reason, having the blade so close to her skin didn't worry her when it was Mateo doing the cutting. Maybe it was because the touch of his fingers on her skin as he moved them down her leg distracted her from being scared. "Rule number one is to get the hell out of any collapsed building ASAP. Which you're going to do right now, to get a crew down here with a stretcher. I'm surprised someone hasn't already come in here."

"Okay." She knew he was right, that trying to move John, even with his injury splinted and in a sling, would be painful and dangerous if he had to try to walk, especially after all the blood he'd lost. "I'll be right back."

"Back?" His focus was on finishing tying the last strip over the book then fashioning a sling from her scarf, but his scowl was most definitely directly at her. "Don't be stupid. Just tell them where we are."

And again he was right. Why she was feeling this weird need to actually see both of them make it out, she didn't know. But she wasn't needed here, and might well be needed at the hospital. "Okay," she repeated as she stood, ridiculously feeling a need to brush some of the powdery dirt from her coat. "Since I definitely am not stupid, I'll see you at—"

"Anybody in here?"

Miranda sagged in relief at the voices and the sight of two bobbing flashlights.

"Back here! About thirty feet. Bring a stretcher," Mateo called. "Just one victim. No access to the subway platform. He came in because he was trying to get his dog out."

"Got a stretcher right outside." In mere moments two medics were there, Mateo helping them get John settled on the stretcher as he shared details of the patient's condition and treatment. They wore full gear—reflective coats, hard hats, gloves, and various tools dangled from their belts. Which made Miranda wonder, for the first time, why Mateo was in street clothes. Or, actually, at that moment, very few clothes, with his shirt destroyed and his coat still off, and she found herself staring at his wide, muscled chest and broad shoulders.

"Are you off duty?" she asked.

"Yes. I was on my way to the main collapse when I saw John run in after Benny, then get hit by a chunk of concrete."

"My little dog…" The two men picked up the stretcher, ready to carry him out, and John's words were bitten off as he moaned.

"You get out of here too, Mateo," one of the rescuers said. "You're not equipped. I'll send some guys in to check for anyone else, just in case, but the good news is that it looks like a structural collapse, nothing else. We've got plenty of crew on the scene and if no one else is in here, that means everyone's out and clear both places. So you can go on home."

"I have make sure a certain stubborn doctor gets to the hospital first."

"Tough job you have," one said, laughing, as they made their way toward daylight.

Miranda bent to casually retrieve her purse and flashlight from the ground, not wanting to show him how eager she was to get the heck out of there now that John was taken care of.

Not wanting him to see how she'd been staring at his beautiful body. "You know, I'm not stubborn. It just seemed like I should help if I could, just like you did."

"It's my job to run into harm's way when necessary. Don't think that's in your job description. Come on."

He slid the filthy coat back on over his naked torso, then reached for her elbow. As they stepped over chunks of concrete, Miranda suddenly longed to be outside in the cold air and out of the dark gloom. Which she wouldn't admit to Mateo for the world. "You don't need to hold me up. I'm perfectly capable—"

"I just want to get outside, and if you fall and gash open your head we'll be stuck in here all that much longer."

"I'm sorry if I've made the situation more difficult," she said, her stomach churning a little that he seemed to still think she'd done exactly that, and what did that make her? A pain in the neck, that's what, just like her stepmother had told her for years. "I should have thought it through better and gotten a firefighter instead of coming in here myself."

"Yes, you should've. But I have to admire how brave you are. And you were a big help, even though I hate to admit it."

Even in the darkness she could see the smile

in his eyes, which put a warm little glow in her chest and had her smiling back.

"That's much better than telling me I'm annoying and stubborn," she said. "You—"

A deep, ground-shaking rumble was followed instantly by sharp cracks and the thud of chunks of concrete hitting the ground. Miranda gasped, instinctively covering her head with her arms, as though that flimsy barrier could protect her in any way, when a heavy weight slammed straight into her.

CHAPTER TWO

MATEO'S HARD BODY took her down like a football linebacker, as he somehow managed to wrap his arms around her before they hit the earth. The sharp pebbles they landed on stabbed and scraped her one bare leg, a bigger chunk of concrete jabbed into her ribs, and her face landed on the hard pillow of Mateo's muscled forearm before sliding off it into a pile of silty debris.

His weight smashed her down so hard she couldn't get her mouth clear to breathe, and his body jerked at the same time as he grunted loudly in her ear. Lifting her head half an inch to suck in a chokingly dusty breath, she twisted and pushed at him, blinded by the dirt in her eyes, which sent tears streaming down her cheeks. "Get off! Can't breathe…"

He didn't move, and she jabbed her elbow into his ribs, which sent another low grunt into her ear. "Hold still a minute," he said. "I just took a boulder for you and you're trying to hurt me more?"

"What?" His weight lifted slightly off her, and she twisted around fully to lie on her back, sucking in deep breaths as she stared up at his grim face. Her hands decided on their own to grab at him, landing inside his coat on his shoulders, clinging, pulling him close. Somehow, she wriggled enough to move her spine off whatever was currently lodged there.

"You okay?"

"I— I'm okay." She realized that was true, she was fine, possibly only because she had a two-hundred-pound blanket of bone and muscle covering her. "You?"

"Bleeding, but okay. And see? Seems to be all finished," he said in a ridiculously calm voice. He lifted his gaze to scan the tunnel. "Let's give this a few more seconds to make sure it's done, then we'll get the hell out of here."

Light silt still showering down in intermittent swishes mingled with his heavy breaths against her lips, and her own fast breathing against his. Their eyes met and held, and she was suddenly acutely aware of the feel of his skin against her palms, the strength of his muscles, the movement of his naked chest against her. The grip she had on his warm shoulders loosened, and her hands moved down his pectorals, smoothing across the soft hair covering them before she realized with dismay what she was doing. Making herself let go, she curled her fingers into her palms to keep from touching him again. Fought the peculiar combination of sensations swirling around her belly that didn't seem connected to the fear that had consumed her just moments before.

She pulled in another deep breath. What in the world? The two of them were lying in a collapsed tunnel, for heaven's sake, and it was long past time to get safe.

"I'm… I'm ready," she said unsteadily. "To leave."

"Finally?" His lips curved just a little. "Let's go."

His big body lifted from hers, and his hands grasped her waist, effortlessly swinging her to her feet. His arm wrapped around her shoulders as they moved quickly out of the tunnel toward the light. Miranda blinked at the brightness of the sky—how had it seemed so gray and gloomy before? The fresh, cold air filled her lungs, sharp and stinging and wonderful. Trembling a little now that the whole thing was over, she tried not to think about how bad it could have turned out, and turned to see Mateo watching her with an odd expression on his face.

"You sure you're okay?"

Probably, she looked pale and shaken, her pretense of bravery through the situation now shot to heck. "Yes, okay. Thanks for, you know, crushing me with your body so I didn't get crushed worse by flying debris."

"You're welcome. Except I didn't completely succeed. Your coat is torn."

She followed his gaze to the large rip in the shoulder seam of her coat, and couldn't help the little dismayed sound that came from her lips. "Oh, no! I just bought this last month! Must have happened when you tackled me."

"Better a torn coat than a broken head. Which you would have deserved for not leaving when I asked you to."

"Not even I deserve a broken head."

That statement made his lips quirk as he reached out to brush his finger across her dusty eyelids. "You'd better get washed up."

"Me? You look like a gray-haired old man right now." Which couldn't be further from the truth, since no old man had the kind of wide, muscular chest that was mostly bare right in front of her, or flat, rippling abs, or such a chiseled jaw. And because she couldn't stop looking at him and was enjoying their banter far too much, she forced herself to look away up the sidewalk, pretending to focus on all the emergency equipment and personnel. Then her peripheral vision caught bright red drops of blood splattering on the sidewalk behind his feet.

Wide-eyed, she jerked her attention back to him. "You're bleeding! Oh, my God."

"I can tell it's just a scrape. Maybe a gouge, too, but nothing worse than that."

"Take off your coat so I can see."

"I'll freeze."

"Better to freeze than die from blood loss." She pushed at the shoulders of his open coat and, shaking his head and grumbling, he finally slid it off. She turned him around, then stared in dismay at the swollen, raw scrape and shallow puncture wound that was the source of the drops of blood. "For heaven's sake, you really did take a boulder for me!"

"I'll live."

"Does it hurt anywhere else?" She ran her hands across his shoulders and back, wiping off the dusty debris from when he'd had his coat off earlier, looking for other injuries that might not be obvious. "I feel just terrible that I was pushing and jabbing you to get off me when you really were hurt."

"Like I said, just a scrape. And I'm tough."

He tried to turn around, but she stopped him. "And you call me stubborn! Just be still a minute." With her scarf gone, the best she could do to staunch the trickle of blood was a pathetic wad of tissue she scrounged from her coat pocket, pressing it firmly against the bruised indentation as her left hand continued to roam his hard contours and smooth skin.

Abruptly and without warning, he surprised her by turning, her hands moving along with him, and the sight of that manly chest and the feel of his skin and soft hair on her palms had her mesmerized again, touching him the same way she'd touched his back, slowly and thoroughly, though there was clearly no injury on this side of his body.

"You about finished examining me, Doctor?"

Oh, my God. His low rumble made her realize exactly what she'd been doing. Dropping the tissue and yanking her hands back like she'd touched a hot furnace, horrified that she'd practically been fondling the man, she stared up at amused brown eyes.

"I'm sorry... I didn't mean to, you know, run my hands all over you like that, I was just, um, checking for more injuries, but you seem..." She cleared her throat, utterly mortified. "Fine."

He gave her a slow smile that said he knew exactly why she'd been touching him, which had been way too softly and leisurely to be considered a medical necessity. Heat flooded her face because, yes, the man was very, very fine and she'd just made an utter fool of herself.

Beyond relieved that he slid his coat back on, she wished with all her heart that he'd button it up, too, so she wouldn't have to keep finding other things to look at. Like his gorgeous face.

"Thanks for the first aid." He reached out to gently smooth a finger down her dirty cheek. "You're a mess. Do you live nearby?"

"No, I live in Brooklyn. But I'll go to the hospital and use the showers there."

"Be careful walking—looks like some of the sidewalk has heaved in the collapse."

He turned and, astonishingly, it looked like he was about to head back inside the collapsed street they'd just come from. "What are you doing?"

"I've got to find John's dog."

"What? Surely you're not going back in there! Or at least get the safety equipment and hard hat on before you do."

"Unless he somehow got out, it won't take long. The space beyond where John was injured ends just another thirty-five feet or so back."

And with that, he disappeared, leaving her with her hands clutched to her chest and her mouth gaping open after him.

What should she do now? Go on to the hospital like she didn't know the crazy man had gone back into harm's way? Go tell the first responders that one of their men was insane? She felt bad about John's poor dog and understood why he'd gone back in for it, but what if the whole ceiling collapsed and neither one of them survived? He should have gotten help before going back in to look for him, and protected himself somehow.

She stood there with various horrible scenarios running through her mind, each worse than the last, making her feel a little woozy. After several minutes ticked by she decided, nearly hyperventilating, that she had to tell someone so that he wouldn't be in there alone, knocked unconscious by a slab of concrete or buried under a shower of rubble, and just as she was about to rush to one of the fire trucks, an even more dusty Mateo trudged up out of the wreckage. A small dog was tucked into the crook of his elbow like a football, and Miranda wasn't sure if she wanted to laugh or yell at him.

She planted her hands on her hips and sucked in a shaky breath. "Are you out of your mind? You had me worried to death!"

"Unnecessary. But when a beautiful woman worries about me, it's appreciated nonetheless." He held up what she could now see was a rather chubby dachshund that was probably brown, though it was hard to tell for sure. "Benny likes it, too, don't you, buddy?" Mateo scratched beneath the dog's chin, who managed to feebly wag his tail despite his ordeal.

Miranda smoothed her hand across the pup's

back, smearing the dust around, and her fear and desire to yell at Mateo faded into a smile of her own. "He's so cute. John will be very glad. How in the world did you find him?"

He stuck two fingers into his mouth, and the shrill whistle was so loud it made Benny squirm and Miranda cover her ears.

"Oh, my gosh! That would make me run instead of come to you. And you do realize your hands are filthy."

"Eating a little dirt is good for one's immune system, which you surely know, Dr. Davenport."

"Yes. Well, I already ate my quota of dirt for the day." Aware of a ridiculous desire to just stand there and talk with him for hours, filthy and cold or not, she managed to remember that she had to see if the hospital had a big patient load after the collapse. "Gotta go. You want me to find John and tell him? What are you going to do with the dog?"

"Take him home. I'll call the hospital and have them tell John, and he can find someone to come pick him up."

"That's…nice of you." In spite of her best intentions, her eyes kept wandering from the dog to Mateo's naked chest beneath his coat, remembering how his skin and body had felt, and she decided she'd better get out of there before he could see exactly what she was thinking. "Well…"

Fixated as she was on his handsome face and beautiful physique, she didn't even hear the chime of her cellphone announcing a text until his finger pointed to her purse. "That your phone?"

"Oh! Yes. Thanks." Lord, had he noticed her distractedly, ridiculously, staring at his body? Again? She quickly fished in her bag and read the message. "The hospital says they don't need me. That there aren't too many injured, they're sure it wasn't a terrorist event, and everything's under control. So that's good news."

"It is."

She lifted her eyes to his brown ones, and something about the way he was looking at her made her chest suddenly feel oddly buoyant. The thought of going to her apartment and being all alone for the rest of the day pushed that air right back out, but she shook it off. When she wasn't working, didn't she spend most of her time alone anyway?

"Well, good luck with the dog and all." She cleared her throat. "See you at the hospital sometime."

She turned away from that mesmerizing brown gaze and started walking, then realized she'd have to rethink her route, since the subway she usually rode might be out of commission. She pulled up the subway updates on her phone to check which ones were running and which weren't, when a large, dirty hand rested on her forearm to stop her in her tracks.

"So where are you going?" Mateo asked.

"Brooklyn. My subway might be open but if not, I'll just take a taxi."

"In this mess? It'll take you hours."

And wasn't that the truth? The clogged-up traffic looked even worse than when she'd left the taxi. "Then I'll go to the hospital after all."

"Do you have a friend or boyfriend who lives close enough to walk to their place?"

"No boyfriend, and most of my family live on the Upper East Side."

"I live just a couple of blocks from here. You might as well come with me and Benny and get cleaned up there. I probably have pants that'll fit you that you could wear home."

She'd hardly be surprised if a man as hunky as Mateo Alves had clothes women had left at his place, but she wasn't about to wear any of them. "Thanks, but no. I'll be fine."

"Suit yourself. Walking ten blocks to the hospital, covered with dirt, wearing a torn coat and pants with one bare leg exposed in this cold, is going to feel very uncomfortable." An indifferent shrug made her wonder why he was even asking. "And if you can ride the subway, people will think you're homeless and want to sit far away from the strangely dusty woman with ripped clothes. Or offer you money."

She had to laugh at that, but as she looked down at herself, she realized he was right. Not to mention that her leg already felt a little numb from the cold wind. And what if she ran into someone she knew, or a former patient, and had to answer a gazillion questions and have people think she was crazy to run into a collapsed tunnel, just like Mateo had?

She thought about how her sister Penny always accused her of doing everything in her life as safely as possible, and today she'd proved that wasn't always true. And taking Mateo up on his offer would definitely not be the quiet, boring route either, would it?

"Fine." Her pulse quickened as she agreed. "I appreciate it."

"I have a secret reason for asking, you realize."

Her heart lurched at the wicked glint that suddenly appeared in his eyes, and a whole lot of possibilities swirled through her head. Was she out of her mind to actually go with him? Her eyes glued to his, she breathlessly asked, "What?"

"Benny can't be returned in his current condition." He held out the little dog. "I'm hoping you'll take him in the shower with you to get him washed up as well."

* * *

Miranda felt warm from head to toe as she shoved her arms into the oversized white robe Mateo had given her before her shower. She had a bad feeling that the heat pumping from her pores was from more than just the hot shower. That it might have something to do with feeling embarrassed that she was naked in Mateo Alves's bathroom, and that she'd been thinking thoughts that should not have formed in her brain at all.

Thoughts of Mateo coming into the small space while she was in the shower, which of course would be horrifying and creepy in real life. But in her fantasy world, safe behind a locked bathroom door? Very, very exciting. And what woman wouldn't think about that for at least a second, when the man was the most gorgeous male specimen she'd ever laid eyes on?

Not to mention that there was something about him that made her feel utterly safe. Had even felt absurdly safe in that tunnel with debris showering down on them, which was ridiculous. His body, big though it was, couldn't have fully shielded her if the entire street had collapsed on them. But that he'd thrown himself on her to protect her the best he could made her feel a little warm glow, even though she knew it was part of his job and he'd been angry with her for even being there in the first place.

She stared into the mirror and finger-combed her damp hair, glad she'd decided to cut it into a bob a couple of years ago. With her work schedule it was easier to take care of now, and after today's crazy events it would have been a tangled mess if it had been longer. She shook her head at the sudden wish that she had more than just lipstick, making a mental note to put some makeup in her purse for next time.

As though there'd be another time she'd rush into danger, be yelled at by the world's most handsome paramedic, then insistently brought to his home to get cleaned up. No, this was a once-in-a-lifetime moment, and she needed to get her clothes dried fast and get out of there before she embarrassed herself again by ogling him. Before he remembered he'd been annoyed about her getting in his way today. The kind of annoyance she'd gotten all too used to once Vanessa Davenport had grudgingly allowed her to live with her father and half-siblings.

"Thanks again for your robe," she said as she walked into his small but comfortable living room, tying the attached terrycloth belt of the over-large robe even tighter. She stared at him lounging on his sofa and licked her dry lips, trying to sound calm and normal instead of absurdly nervous. Which was obviously a ridiculous way for a mature woman to feel, but boyfriends had been few and far between in her life, mostly because she'd quickly learned that none of them had been interested in her, just in her name and the Davenport money and connections. "Are my...are my clothes almost dry?"

"They need maybe ten more minutes." Unfolding his body from the deep leather sofa, he moved toward the bathroom with Benny, now wrapped in a towel to keep the dust from getting everywhere, tucked under his arm again. "I hope you left some hot water for us."

Her mouth went even dryer. "You're...going to shower? Now?"

Dark eyebrows lifted at her as he paused. "Do you object to me using my own shower? I believe I'm covered in even more silt than you were. And I can't exactly pass Benny on in his current state, since you refused to take him in with you."

"Of course I don't object." Which was a lie, because she really wanted to say, *Yes! I'd really rather you wait to take off your clothes until after I'm gone!* "And I didn't refuse, you said you'd take care of washing him."

"Because I'm an excellent dog washer, and I suspect you don't have much experience with canines."

It was true, but the way he said it seemed

to imply he thought she was a prima donna or something. "You sure do claim to be excellent at everything. And I'm sure I could handle washing a little dog."

"I have no doubt you handle all kinds of things with aplomb, Dr. Davenport." That quick grin of his flashed before he disappeared into the only bedroom.

Apparently, she'd fooled him pretty well, because there was only one thing she was really good at, and that was being a doctor. Something she'd worked hard to do, trying to live up to the Davenport name. The family she only sort of belonged to, and would probably never be worthy of.

The sound of the bathroom door clicking behind him sent Miranda to perch on the end of the sofa, looking around his small apartment. His decor could be described as minimalist, but the furniture was obviously expensive, and the few pieces of art unusual and eclectic. Not posters from a cheap store but beautifully framed originals hung on the walls, and several excellent sculptures were placed on the modern tables.

She ran her finger across a bronze with fluid lines. Interesting and unexpected that an EMT would have the financial resources for art like this. Maybe he was the kind of man who bought very little, but when he did, it was only the best.

Pondering the man, she absently picked up a magazine, surprised to see that it was about horses and horse-breeding, and flicked through the photos of beautiful animals, hoping for a distraction from her nerves. Until the sound of the shower put a completely different image in her head. Picturing a naked, muscular Mateo with water streaming down the dark hair on his chest shortened her breath and did other things to her body that embarrassed her all over again, reminding her of exactly how she'd felt in that tunnel when he'd been lying on top of her.

Lord, this was ridiculous. What in the world was wrong with her? She was twenty-nine years old, for heaven's sake, and a doctor who'd seen plenty of naked men in her career. Naked men were in her life every day!

Except Mateo wasn't a patient, and she couldn't remember a single man she'd ever known, patient or otherwise, who'd been even close to as gorgeous as he was.

She blew out a breath, and just as she was about to go to the small laundry closet to check on her clothes and throw them on, damp or not, a loud knock sounded at the door to his apartment.

She stared, frozen. Should she answer? The distant sound of the shower told her Mateo wasn't even close to being done, and if she hadn't been there, he wouldn't be answering anyway, right?

Besides, what if it was a girlfriend or something? How could she explain being in his apartment in his robe? Then she remembered it might be whoever was coming to get Benny, and decided she'd better answer before they left, assuming no one was home. She moved toward the door as a man's voice boomed through it.

"Mateo! Are you there?"

To Miranda's surprise, she heard the keypad beep just before the doorknob turned. The door opened to reveal an older couple, probably in their early sixties. The petite woman had dark hair with streaks of gray, coiffed into an elegant chignon, and the man was tall and unusually slender. He held a cane and was walking slowly, a step behind the woman as they came into the apartment. Both stared at her with raised eyebrows as their gazes took in her wet hair and the fact that she was standing there naked except for Mateo's robe.

The embarrassment she'd felt before flamed another hundred degrees, and if there'd been anywhere she could have run, she would have torn right out of there.

"Is Mateo here?" the woman asked, her eyes remarkably cold-looking for being a warm, velvety brown.

"Um, yes. He's…he's in the shower. See, there was an accident today, part of the subway tunnel collapsed, you might have seen it on the news, or gotten stuck in all the traffic? So I went to help and Mateo was in there rescuing a man and his dog, and we got all dirty, and then…" Her voice faded away. Lord, she must sound like a raving lunatic. "Um, come in. I'm sure he'll be out in—"

"Mother. Father. What are you doing here? I thought you'd already left for home."

Miranda turned to see Mateo standing in the doorway to his bedroom, and what little breath she had left backed up in her lungs. Because he was wearing a towel around his waist and nothing else, with a sheen of water droplets in relief on his wide shoulders and athletic chest, a few dripping down the dark hair on his taut stomach just as she'd visualized earlier. Only even better.

She gulped. Obviously, he'd heard voices and hadn't taken the time to fully dry off, and between the vision in front of her and her embarrassment that these two people were his *parents*, she thought she just might go into a swoon.

"Our plane is ready to go, but we decided to come here before we left, hoping to convince you to come home with us now, instead of waiting. But apparently you are otherwise engaged."

His mother turned those cold eyes to Miranda, and they reminded her so much of the way her stepmother had always looked at her, it made her heart constrict oddly. Made her feel as unwelcome as she had in her teens when she'd first shown up at the Davenport mansion, which was absurd. She didn't even know these people, but she couldn't help feeling like she'd somehow shoved herself somewhere she was unwelcome anyway.

Mateo folded his arms across his damp chest, his features stony. "I told you I'd be coming home soon. And I will."

"It must be very soon. There are things we need to address right away. You are the heir now!" His father pulled a sheaf of papers from his coat pocket and held them out to Mateo, his hand shaking with what looked to be a tremor as he did so. "Your mother and I are trying to manage until you arrive, but it is difficult for us to attend to everything. Too many people are relying on me, on you, to be ignored."

Miranda looked from Mateo to his parents, and back. What in the world were they talking about? Unlike his mother, his father's attention was focused exclusively on Mateo, who made no effort to introduce her to them. Which shouldn't have bothered her, except it made her feel even more like the lowly interloper that Vanessa Davenport had clearly viewed her as thirteen years ago. And still did.

"I understand. I'll let you know when I'm going to arrive, which I promise will be in just a few days." Mateo's biceps bulged as he lifted his arm to squeeze the back of his neck, his expression grim. A now clean, tail-wagging Benny ran from the bedroom to stand next to Mateo's feet, looking up at him adoringly as Mateo dropped his arm back to his side. "However, as you can see, I'm rather busy right now."

"You have a dog? In this ridiculously tiny apartment you insist on living in?" his mother asked in an incredulous voice.

"It's not my dog."

A man of few words. Miranda had to wonder about the odd exchange between Mateo and his parents, with him obviously not wanting to share anything about the events of the day. It was also obvious they weren't going to be sharing warm and fuzzy hugs. She knew how it felt to have a strained relationship with your own family, and hoped it didn't bother him the way her own situation always had.

"Well. We will see you at home, then, and look forward to your arrival."

His mother's eyes rested on Miranda one more time before she turned and swept out into the hallway without another word, her husband slowly following. It struck Miranda that their bearing was remarkably regal, their clothes obviously expensive. It was somehow surprising that these two unusually elegant people had a

son whose chosen profession was that of a paramedic. But as she watched Mateo move to close
the door behind them, it struck her that there
was something intangibly noble about his bearing too.

He turned, his face impassive. "Sorry about
that. Probably your clothes are ready."

His words reminded her that she was still
standing there in his robe, otherwise naked, and
that he was practically naked, too. She found herself staring again at the beyond sexy contours of
his torso, the beautiful golden shade of his skin,
and the dark hair covering his pectorals and hard
stomach, which she knew felt soft to the touch.
Jerking her eyes up to his didn't help the breathless feeling that came over her, as they only managed to land on his chiseled jaw and the beautiful
shape of his unsmiling mouth, and her own lips
parted to suck in a much-needed breath.

What was it about Mateo Alves that had her
feeling so peculiarly stirred up and uncomfortable and embarrassingly aroused whenever he
was near?

One hand lifted to clutch her robe tighter to
her throat before he turned to get her clothes
from his small laundry closet. Eyeing the wound
on his back as he opened the dryer, she nearly
offered to bandage it for him in case it started
bleeding again, but decided she needed to keep

her hands off his body. Getting dressed and out of there as soon as possible was the best plan, and she practically snatched the warm clothes he brought from the dryer.

"There are a pair of women's sweatpants on my bed for you. It's the best I could do."

"Anything is better than walking down the street with only one pants leg," she said, feeling a little strange about wearing pants that had presumably belonged to a lover of his, but she didn't have much choice. "I'll get dressed, then out of your hair."

Finally respectably covered up, she swiped on a little lipstick, still feeling oddly jittery as she went back to his living room.

"Thanks again for letting me get pulled together here. I guess I'll see you around the hospital sometime."

"Are you feeling all right?" The way he was carefully looking at her made her wonder what he was seeing. "Not stressed or odd about having concrete showering down on you, wondering if it was going to get worse? It's okay if you do. Even after regularly being in harm's way, plenty of people suffer emotional aftereffects from it."

"Well, as you pointed out, it's pretty much my own fault for going in there to begin with. Makes you think about how quickly things can happen, doesn't it? I see the results of bad accidents in the hospital every day, but somehow I never think about it happening to me."

"So next time promise you'll stay put and get someone trained in search and rescue."

"I'm hoping there's no 'next time.' But I can't promise—I took an oath to help sick or injured people, and if I have to put myself in harm's way, I'm going to do it."

"Yep, a very stubborn woman." A small smile curved his lips even as he shook his head in exasperation. "Just be sure to take care of yourself, and if you start to have bad dreams or flashbacks, talk to someone about it."

"Don't worry, I really am fine. But thanks." Maybe he thought she sounded stubborn and brave, but the truth was, she fervently hoped she never came across another situation like that in her life. "I do have vacation time coming up this week. I'm planning to get out of the city, do something fun."

"Like what?"

"Still figuring that out." The main reason to go away was so she didn't have to be at the big Thanksgiving family gathering at the Davenports'. She shoved her hand toward his, and his warm one engulfed hers. "Goodbye, and thanks again."

The way she rushed out of his apartment probably made him wonder if she really did have some post-traumatic stress going on, but she couldn't worry about that. She had enough to worry about.

Like what she was going to do with her week off, and why she'd had a sudden, astonishing urge to ask Mateo Alves to join her.

CHAPTER THREE

THE CHILD'S PIERCING shrieks would have unnerved even the most hardened EMT, and Mateo
stepped up the pace to get her into the ER fast.
Based on what the father had told him when he'd
picked the wailing child up off the sidewalk, it
seemed unlikely she had an internal injury. No
blood, no visible head injury, no misshapen limb
told him it probably wasn't extremely serious.
But because he couldn't know for sure, that's
why they were heading to the hospital—to check
out the possibilities then go from there.

The anxious father had agitatedly told him the
story of how the three-year-old girl had been sitting on his shoulders as they'd walked through
the crowds. The dad hadn't expected his daughter to suddenly lunge sideways to get a better
look at a toy store's glittering Christmas window display, and he'd lost his grip on her legs.

"I just couldn't catch her all the way, you
know?" the father repeated as Mateo and the

other EMT lifted the stretcher out of the ambulance. "I partially broke her fall to the sidewalk, but I'm so scared she might be really hurt."

"I know it's scary," Mateo said in a calm voice he hoped would keep the poor guy from hyperventilating. "But Manhattan Mercy's ER docs are the best so, whatever's going on, they'll figure it out. Try not to worry."

The man nodded and gulped in some air, and Mateo turned to his patient. "Almost there, Emily," he said, giving the girl an encouraging smile. "Soon the doctors will figure out why you're hurting and get you something for your pain, okay?"

"What do you think is wrong?" the girl's father asked. Apparently, Mateo's attempts to reassure him weren't working. His voice was panicky, and his knuckles were white as he hung onto the gurney Mateo propelled through the ER's doorway. "It…it didn't look like she hit her head, but I couldn't tell for sure, you know?"

"Her vital signs are normal, other than an accelerated heart rate, probably caused by pain. I'm guessing it's not anything major, but we'll have the doctor take a look." Hopefully, whoever the doctor was would do a better job calming the dad than he'd managed to accomplish.

A nurse sent them to an exam room, and when a white-coated doctor with chin-length brown hair appeared in Mateo's peripheral vision, he knew it was Miranda Davenport before he'd even looked up. As if he'd somehow sensed it was her, and how strange was that? Also strange that he couldn't help the smile that formed on his face just from seeing her again.

"Hi," Miranda said with a sweet smile as she came to lean over the child and give her a comforting pat. "What's going on?"

"Three-year-old girl fell from her dad's shoulders onto the sidewalk." Mateo began his report as he unbuckled her from the gurney. Being careful to not jostle her, he gently moved her to the bed. "Ambulatory at the scene. Heart rate one twenty, BP ninety over fifty. Her name is Emily, and this is her father."

"What do you think, Doctor?"

The man's anxious eyes stared at Miranda, and Mateo decided that the professional but still warm smile she gave him would have had anyone breathing slightly easier. "We're about to find out," Miranda said as she turned that smile to Emily. "I know you're hurting, but can you be brave for me? Just like the princess here always is?"

Miranda tapped the sticker of a glittery cartoon princess she had attached to her name badge, and, remarkably, the child nodded and hiccupped as her crying lessened a little.

"Wow, you really are brave, like her! So, can you tell me where you hurt?"

The child waved her left hand toward the right side of her body, and Miranda moved her hands gently over Emily's head, then her arms and torso. Her careful fingers slowly went to touch Emily's neck, and Mateo instantly saw the swelling forming there. The child shrieked again, and Miranda lifted her head, her gaze meeting Mateo's for a long moment before moving on to the child's father.

"It looks like she has a fractured clavicle. See the bulge here on her collar bone? That might not sound like good news since she's hurting so much, but it's a comparatively simple injury that will heal well on its own. We'll get her pain meds right away to make her comfortable, then an X-ray to confirm the diagnosis. But I'm sure that's what the problem is."

That smile, her quick diagnosis, her ability to calm the child and her father, and the utter confidence illuminating her amazing blue eyes, all wrapped up in what Mateo knew was a hell of an attractive body, were one irresistible package.

"Thank God it's nothing super-bad," Emily's father said, swiping his hand across his brow. "What can you do for it? My wife is probably gonna kill me. I really need to know what to tell her when she calls me back."

"We'll get her a sling called a clavicle strap to keep her arm and shoulder from moving as it heals. And you can tell your wife that it's very common for young children to fracture their clavicles, sometimes even from a simple fall in their own homes. So she's actually a pretty tough cookie, aren't you, Emily?"

The child sniffled between whimpering cries and nodded as Miranda pulled one of the princess stickers from her coat pocket and handed it to Emily. "I hope this will always remind you how brave you were today. Your mom and dad should be proud of you."

Another nod, and as Emily even managed to smile through her sniffles this time, Mateo realized that Miranda had a special gift for soothing little ones.

"You don't put a cast or anything on it?" the father asked.

"If the two ends of the broken clavicle are in the same state, I promise it will heal on its own." Miranda sent the man another encouraging smile before giving instructions to the nurse about not moving Emily's arm or shoulder, and what pain medication to give her.

Mateo's job was done here, and though he would have liked to stay a little longer to watch Miranda work her magic, he figured he should get the ambulance back to the station. He pushed the gurney from the room, but as he passed Miranda in the hallway, she paused in typing her instructions into the computer chart and turned to look at him.

"Busy day?"

"Not too bad. No collapsed tunnels with crazy doctors running inside."

"Or dusty dogs to deal with." Her lips curved. "Did John's family come and get Benny?"

"Yes. My apartment seemed quiet after the little guy was gone."

"So getting a dog might be on your to-do list?"

"Probably not." He had other things on that list. Like being forced to move back home when he didn't want to, despite being needed there, and the guilt of his feelings about all that gnawed at his gut. He couldn't tell his parents he didn't deserve to step into his brother's shoes to take over the family's estate full-time. That his not being there for Emilio, for not doing more to help him, might be part of the reason he wasn't alive anymore. That memories of his laughter and jokes, of their closeness and all they'd done together their whole lives, were a constant ache every moment he was back in Spain.

The weight of all that hung heavily on his shoulders, as it had for the past six months, and he didn't know what he was going to do about it. Didn't know how he could convince his parents that it would be fine for him to be home just a few months of the year, when they expected him to be there full-time now that Emilio was gone.

As he stared at Miranda's pretty face and smiling eyes and thought about the disapproving looks his parents had given her, a radical idea struck him, slowly forming fully in his mind. And the more he thought about it, the more he liked it.

Yes, it just might be brilliant, and actually work. But would she possibly agree? He had no idea. But what he did know? Trying to persuade her just became the number one thing on that to-do list.

By the end of the day, Mateo had become convinced that the idea that had developed in his head earlier was the perfect solution to his problem. If Miranda was willing to go along with it, that was.

After all, what did he have to lose by asking her? He definitely couldn't suggest it to one of the women he casually dated, because they might read more into it than he wanted them to. But since he and Miranda barely knew one another, he couldn't imagine she'd read his proposal the wrong way. Plus, she was a Davenport. Someone from a wealthy and powerful family wouldn't think his lineage was a big deal and because of that, she'd be unlikely to get excited about it, like the women back at home always had. Women who wanted nothing more than to snag a wealthy duke, live a lavish lifestyle, and lord it over everyone who worked for his family, like his sister-in-law had.

Which was just one of the reasons he liked living anonymously in a big city like New York. He could date women for a short time who didn't want anything from him. No long-term commitments offered or expected, and that's how he wanted to keep it.

Miranda had said she didn't have a boyfriend, which he found incredibly surprising, but was more than glad about. She had also said that she'd like to get out of the city for a week or so. Get away from work and the challenges of getting to her apartment while the subway was being repaired. Away from memories of the tunnel collapse and how scary he knew that had to have been for her, even though she'd put on a brave front.

He thought about that again while he waited around for her shift to end. Frustrated with her as he'd been at that moment, now that she was safe and it was over with he had to admire that she'd run in there to help. Search and rescue had been his passion since his days in the Spanish military, but she lived her life on the receiving end of casualties in the ER. Without a doubt, lots of physicians would have waited for the rescue crews to bring out any injured before they got to work taking care of them.

He leaned against the wall of the hospital corridor, his gaze on Miranda standing farther down the hall, talking to the doctor taking over her patients. Did she always take this long to tie up loose ends after her shift was over? He glanced at his watch, impressed that, unlike some of the docs in the hospital who ran out the door the second their shift was over, she obviously wanted to make sure everyone was taken care of before she left.

Restlessly squeezing the back of his neck, he wondered if there was any way she'd agree to his proposal. If she said no, he'd just be in the same situation he was in now, right? But maybe he'd get lucky and she'd say yes, which would solve his problem at least in the short term. At the same time, he'd get to look at her pretty face and enjoy her lively mind during the time they spent together.

He'd always taken a second and third look at her whenever he'd brought in a patient, never dreaming he'd have her lush body beneath his the way it had been in the tunnel, or her nearly naked in his apartment. The memories of how both those things had made his blood pump hard and his breath get short had him turning to look somewhere other than at her before his body reacted all over again.

Miranda finally headed to the locker room and emerged just a few minutes later. Mateo pushed off the wall and moved toward her, watching as her slender fingers slowly buttoned her coat. She looked deep in thought about something, and he wondered if her brain was working overtime about her patients, or if something else was on her mind.

"Miranda."

She turned, and her amazing blue eyes that had shone through the darkness in that tunnel lifted to his in surprise. "What are you doing here? I thought your shift ended quite a while ago."

"It did. I came to see if you'd like to join me for coffee. A little thank-you for doing such a great job with Emily this afternoon."

"Oh. Well." Her tongue moistened her lips, and he found himself fixating again on how soft and full they were. "I was just doing my job, you know."

"Yes, but you do it very well." She looked so wide-eyed and shocked he couldn't help but tease her a little. "It's just coffee, Miranda. Surely your time in my apartment showed you I'm not a big, bad wolf."

A nervous little laugh left those pretty lips. "No. I mean, yes, I know. Of course, I'd love some coffee."

"Good. How about we go to the coffee house two blocks down? Pardon me for saying so, but the stuff they serve in the hospital is swill."

Another laugh, but this time it was a real one. "I don't mind it. But I suspect those of European heritage are a little more picky than those of us raised in Chicago."

He felt his eyebrows rise. He'd seen the Davenport mansion, and it was in one of the most exclusive areas in New York City. "Chicago? What do you mean? I know you live in Brooklyn now, but didn't you grow up on the Upper East Side?"

"Long story."

He wished he hadn't said anything, because the smile on her face instantly disappeared, and he hoped he hadn't ruined his chances of her going along with his proposal before he'd even had a chance to ask. He grasped her elbow and headed toward the revolving back door. "Come on. It's been a long day for both of us. I don't know about you, but I need a double shot of espresso, *pronto*."

"Espresso pronto sounds like exactly the drink I need right now." The twinkle in her beautiful eyes was new to him, as she'd been so serious during their previous interactions. But he liked it. A lot. "Let's go."

A somewhat private corner table was open, and Mateo steered them there, glad he could ask his important question without anyone overhearing. After some general hospital talk and conversation about the continuing traffic mess from the tunnel collapse, Mateo drew a breath.

It was show time.

"I have something I'd like to talk with you about," he said. "To ask you."

"All right." She looked a little concerned about that, and he wondered what his expression was, forcing himself to relax. Not a big deal, right? Nothing to stress about. She'd either give him a yes or no, and he'd go from there.

"You met my parents yesterday," he said. "They—"

"Actually, I didn't meet them," she interrupted. "You didn't introduce me."

He stared at her, then realized that was true. Their stopping by his apartment unannounced, lambasting him and trying to drag him home right then and there, had upset him so much he'd completely forgotten his manners.

"I'm very sorry. That was rude of me. I was frustrated at the situation, which is what I want to talk to you about."

Her eyes met his, serious again. She sat quietly, sipping her coffee, and something about her expression and the caring way she was looking at him helped him relax.

"I've heard your family described as New York royalty. My family is a little like yours. We have a dukedom in Spain. In Catalonia, about an hour from Barcelona."

"A…what? A dukedom?"

"Sí." He had to smile at her incredulous expression. "I know you may think I'm making up a story, but it's true. You're welcome to look us up on the internet. You'll see my father, Rafael Alves; my mother, Ana Alves; and myself listed under the Duchy of Pinero, living at the Castillo de Adelaide Fernanda. My brother, Emilio, is listed as well." Just saying his name made Mateo's chest constrict with pain and disbelief. It was probably even worse for his parents since Emilio had been the favorite, golden son, which was another reason Mateo could never take his place.

"Wow. That's real royalty, not the fake kind the Davenports enjoy." Her palm pressed against her cheek as she stared at him. "I wondered what in the world your father was saying about you being an heir or something. What made you move to New York, if you had a cushy life of back home?"

Cushy life. If only she knew the difficult dynamics of their family. "I served in the Spanish army for four years, and discovered there my love for search and rescue. For field medicine. Being part of a team. Working as an EMT is a little like that, and I enjoy the anonymity of a big city like New York."

He wouldn't go into all the reasons he'd wanted to leave home, which included despising his brother's cheating, social-climbing wife and Emilio's private pain because of it. Somehow, for as long as possible, he had to avoid being thrust back into that world. Did part of him feel bad about that attitude? Hell, yeah. He also felt horrible that his father's health continued to decline. He had to find some kind of compromise where he could be there for his parents while still living most of the year here. Away from painful memories he didn't want to be reminded of every day.

"But they want you to go back home." She said it as a statement, not a question, which wasn't a surprise, since she'd heard his parents insisting he go back right away.

"Yes. My father is ill and handed over his responsibilities to my brother a few years ago. Then, six months ago, Emilio died in an accident. I became the heir and they believe it's my responsibility to run the estate."

"Oh, Mateo, I'm so sorry. I know how hard it is to lose someone you love."

She placed her warm palm on top of his as her eyes filled with a deep compassion. Remarkable, really, how a blue that intense could be warm and soft and brilliant all at the same time. Normally, he didn't want others' sympathy, but hers felt genuine and so full of caring for a man she barely knew that he found himself soaking it in, despite himself.

"Yes, it's been…hard. And just as hard is the thought that I have to leave my life here. We have many managers at the estate who are good at what they do. If I'm there only part-time, I believe that will be enough."

"You grew up there. Why don't you want to move back?"

"I like my job here. And there are reasons that I've been somewhat isolated from my family for a long time." Despite the question and the way her eyes focused on him in a way that showed she cared, he didn't want to go into them right then. "My father's illness puts pressure on me to step into his shoes, the way Emilio did. While I know that I have to take over for him in some capacity, I'm not going to move back to Spain full-time. I'm confident my parents will come to see that all will be okay when I'm there only part of the year. But I need some time to make that happen, for them to understand that. And that's where you come in."

"Me?"

"Yes, you." He smiled at her expression of startled surprise. "You'd said you have some vacation time and want to get out of the city for a while. I know that, as a Davenport, you have the means to travel anywhere you want, any time. But I can show you the beautiful area of Spain where my family has lived for centuries, have some fun riding our horses. Tour Catalonia and the Pyrenees. At the same time, you can help me accomplish an important goal by doing me a huge favor."

"Goal? Huge favor?" Those intense blue eyes had widened even further, and Mateo drew a fortifying breath, because her saying yes to his proposal suddenly felt much more important than it had an hour ago.

"I'd like for you to pose as my fiancée. My parents won't like me planning to marry an American who doesn't share their culture. I'll tell them you have a contract with the hospital, and can't possibly leave there for another year. You saw their disapproving expressions when you were at my apartment. I'm confident that our faking an engagement would buy me extra time and get them more used to the idea that I'll only be there a few times a year. Please, Miranda?" His heart sped up as he held her hand between his. "Will you pretend to want to marry me?"

* * *

Miranda realized her mouth had sagged open and stayed that way for a very long moment. Managing to finally close it, she stared at Mateo in utter astonishment, unable to find her voice. But who wouldn't be in total shock at his unbelievable proposal?

Pretend to be his fiancée? A fake engagement to keep his parents from insisting he move back right away, while the two of them, two people who barely knew one another, spent vacation time together in Spain? It was the most unbelievable, outrageous thing anyone had ever asked her to do.

And also crazily, absurdly, tempting.

The man was utterly gorgeous. The kind of man any woman would love to spend time with. She'd seen he was caring, too, the way he'd run into the tunnel to help John, and had even put himself in danger again to go back and find Benny. Then today he'd been so good with little Emily, and the synchronized way they'd worked together had been remarkable and impressive.

But all that was a far cry from spending a week with him. And pretending to be engaged, for heaven's sake! Impossible.

"I'm just… I…" She gulped. "I don't even know you, really. That would be too strange, pretending we're, you know, a couple. And going on a trip together. I'm sorry, but I can't."

"I can tell you that it wouldn't be hard for me to pretend to want to spend time with you, because I genuinely do. I know we'd have a good time adventuring together while we're there." He gave her a crooked smile as he squeezed her hand, speaking softly. "When was the last time you did something crazy, Miranda? Just threw caution to the wind? That's what I just did, asking you to pretend to be engaged to me. What do you say? Good or not so good, it will be a true adventure for just a week, right? When we get back, you'll go back to your regular life, as I will, taking with us some enjoyable memories."

When was the last time you did something crazy, Miranda? His words echoed in her head. Her sister Penny lived her life as a daredevil, and had often asked Miranda that question, wondering why she was okay with her life being pretty mundane outside the excitement of the ER. She could just see Penny rolling her eyes at her hesitation, which was part of what had motivated Miranda to be bold and go to Mateo's after the tunnel collapse. How often had her sister challenged her to come along on one of her adventures? Each time she'd refused, Penny had run off without her, shaking her head and grinning, to climb some mountain or abseil from a helicopter or drive a dirt bike on a race course.

When *was* the last time she'd done something crazy? Probably when she'd been sixteen years old, and had gone to see Hugo Davenport, which was a long time ago now. Mostly, she'd lived her life carefully. Sensibly. Studying hard to become a doctor, to try to fit into the Davenport family at least a little. To make them proud of her. She'd excelled at school, and now she mostly worked, still proving herself.

If she'd been looking in a mirror, she could easily see *dull and dutiful* practically tattooed on her forehead.

So wasn't she due for something crazy? Something illogical and inappropriate and completely mad? Something ultra-exciting to do with her week off? After all, when she travelled with her family, she still sometimes felt like the outsider she'd always been. And most of her friends had boyfriends or husbands, and didn't want to vacation without them. So that left Miranda vacationing alone, as she often did.

As she'd planned to do this week. Because she knew that Vanessa Davenport only had a place setting for her at their Thanksgiving table because she was obligated to. And even though Miranda loved her siblings, and knew they cared about her, holidays always reminded her that she didn't really belong the way everyone else did. Having travel plans had become her MO in recent years to avoid that.

Suddenly, the thought of another trip all by her lonesome felt unbearable. Could she really do it? Do something insane and use her vacation time to travel with Mateo? Maybe it would be a disaster, or maybe it would be wonderful, but, no matter which, it would be something she'd never done before, right? Something not careful and sensible and dutiful. And if it turned out to be awkward, it was only one week out of her life. Seven days.

At the same time, she'd be helping Mateo with his problem, and never mind that her friends would tell her she was just being a people-pleaser as usual, which was a learned behavior she'd been trying to work on.

No, Mateo was obviously disconnected from his family, and didn't she know all about feeling that way? The pain he felt over his brother's loss? She had the power to help him during this difficult time. And she couldn't help the thought that, maybe, if she told Vanessa afterwards that she'd been briefly "engaged" to the heir of a dukedom, the woman might actually be slightly impressed.

And how pathetic was it that something like that would even cross her mind?

She drew a breath then stared at the incredibly

handsome man sitting there, smiling encouragingly. "This is…this is the most outrageous thing anyone's ever suggested to me," Miranda said, and the reality of exactly how outrageous it was made her start to laugh. "But I find that, somehow, I can't resist. So my answer is yes, Mateo Alves. Yes, I will go to Spain with you and pretend we're going to get married."

CHAPTER FOUR

MIRANDA WASN'T NEW to flying in a private jet, since the Davenport family often used theirs, and she'd occasionally joined them. So it clearly wasn't the plane departing at night that was making her stomach jump up and down and her heart feel all fluttery.

No, it was the close proximity of the über-sexy man sitting across from her, his deep brown eyes focused on her during the entire take-off. It was the peculiar feeling that, despite the strangeness of the situation, it somehow felt oddly right, too. During the taxi ride to the airport and while they'd been waiting on the tarmac for clearance, he'd talked with her about his work and the ways it intersected with hers. Had shared an amusing story from his childhood that had made her laugh, putting her at ease. He had been an utter gentleman as he took pains to make sure she was comfortable on the plane. He was so proud and regal in his bearing, it struck her that she should have realized he was different from most of the EMTs who brought the injured and ill into Manhattan Mercy's ER.

Her eyes met his and the way he smiled at her had her smiling back, and at the same time her stomach felt oddly squishy, as though she'd known this man for years instead of days.

"Miranda."

His voice made her start. Probably because she'd been fixated on his handsome features and brown eyes and charismatic smile. "Yes?"

"A very small part of me feels a little guilty to have asked you to participate in the charade we are playing. But most of me is very happy that you've agreed to come with me, and I hope you know that. I'm looking forward to spending time with you, and this isn't just about my situation with my parents. So, for all those reasons, thanks for coming with me."

"No need to thank me. I came because I wanted to." And she had. Even when she'd been shocked at his proposal, deep inside she'd wanted to say yes the moment he'd asked, despite the self-protective part of her telling her she shouldn't.

Swatting down those insecure misgivings, she let the excitement of this adventure bubble up in her chest. It overflowed into a big smile she couldn't have stopped even if she'd wanted to.

"We'll be served a late meal soon, then you should try to get some sleep. I'm sure you know that, with the time change, traveling overnight is always best, arriving in the morning refreshed and ready to go."

"I'll try to sleep, but have to confess I'm not good at that."

"Not good at sleeping? What, are you in reality an android?" The corners of his lips tipped up as he raised his eyebrows. "Is this why you seem to always be at the hospital, working?"

She laughed. "No, I'm very human. I just mean I'm not good at sleeping on planes and in cars and such. I just get restless and start thinking too much and then I can't sleep."

"I hope you're not thinking too hard, and worrying, about how our week is going to go. I'll do my best to make it less awkward when dealing with my parents, and show you Catalonia when we're not with them. I can't imagine you not loving it there."

If he felt that way, why was he so determined not to return? "I'm not worrying." Well, truthfully, now that she was actually on this plane with him, she couldn't help but hear, again, those whispers that reminded her she wasn't good enough for a man like Mateo Alves. But it wasn't real, right? So she didn't have to be concerned about not measuring up.

He reached into the pocket of his sport coat, and she stared when he held out what was obviously a small jewelry box, wrapped in light blue paper with a silver ribbon. She looked up to see him giving her an encouraging smile. "Go on, open it."

Oh my gosh. Her breath catching, she carefully tore the paper and lifted open the lid to expose a ring. A ring that held a pale blue stone at its center, surrounded by small white diamonds.

"I…" Miranda swallowed and tried again. "I assume this is a ring you'd like me to wear to convince your parents that we really are engaged?"

"I hope you like it. I got the blue diamond for you to wear because it reminded me of your eyes. Though no stone could look anywhere near as vivid and beautiful."

Her heart oddly fluttered at the seeming sincerity of his words and expression, though at the same time she knew they were probably just the practiced words of a man very good at charming women. "Well, it certainly is…pretty. I'll take good care of it for you."

"Thank you. I had no idea that I'd have to search for a jeweler that would allow me to return a ring. I'd assumed that if the woman said no, that would be a given."

"Well, now you know for up the road when you're asking a woman to marry you for real."

"Trust me, that's never going to happen."

The light amusement on his face disappeared and he turned to look out the window, seeming to concentrate on the gray clouds swirling around the plane. Feeling even more awkward now, Miranda sat there wondering what to do with the ring. Should she put it on, so it was safe on her hand? Or wait until they were about to meet his parents? A part of her wanted to put the dazzling ring on her finger just to see what it would look like there, but that felt too weird. Not that the whole situation wasn't weird. What if everyone at his estate, and not just his parents, took one look at her wearing that and knew she was nowhere near good enough to be a duchess one day? Fake or not, the thought sent a feeling of panic through her lungs that made it hard to breathe.

She swallowed hard and stuck the box in her purse just as Mateo turned to her with another smile that banished his somber look. "One note of warning when it comes to the ring. We have quite a few animals at the castillo, both inside and in the barns. One mischievous Siamese cat we had named Tup Tim was always sneaking onto my mother's dressing table and taking off with any jewelry she'd put there as she was changing.

"Once he stole a diamond bracelet that had belonged to my grandmother, and all of us chased Tup Tim out of the house, all around the grounds, then into the barn, where he ran up to stand on a high beam, triumphantly staring down at us with the bracelet dangling from his mouth. I had to shimmy up a pole and stagger across the beam like a tightrope walker, finally cornering him and retrieving it, and getting bitten for my efforts. He was not happy to lose his prize, but my mother was very pleased with me when I got it back. She never left jewelry on her dressing table again."

The amusing story was just what she'd needed to relax. Had he somehow known?

"That is really funny—I can just picture the scene."

"There was a lot of anxiety on the part of various staff and stable workers as everyone tried to grab the cat, with my mother shouting orders at everyone. I was glad to be the one who succeeded."

Something about the way he'd said his mother had been pleased with him made her wonder if that had been in short supply in his life. She wanted to ask, but decided it wasn't the right time to delve further into the Alves family dynamics.

"I promise not to leave the ring out anywhere, though I admit I'd like to see you tightrope walking."

"Other than getting bitten, I thought it was quite an adventure. I ended up practicing walking along that beam as fast as I could whenever nobody was around to scold me. Turned out to be a good thing. Learning how to do that has come in handy plenty of times during various rescues, believe me."

His flashing grin made her chest feel buoyant all over again. Yes, Penny had been right. Doing something crazy had been the best decision she'd made in a long time. Miranda leaned back in her seat and gave herself up to the pleasure of being on this beautiful plane with smart, gorgeous, and amusing Mateo Alves as her surprise companion for a whole week of adventure she knew would be like nothing she'd ever done before. Nothing serious. Nothing to worry about. Just seven days to enjoy some no-strings fun.

The drive to the family estate was about forty-five minutes from the airport, and now that Miranda was past feeling a little concerned at the speed with which Mateo pushed the sports car through the open, winding roads, she was enjoying every second of the drive. It was more than clear that Mateo was a confident, excellent driver, which allowed her to sit back and soak up the incredible views. Valleys, still green in November, stretched far to the mountains in the distance, only to disappear as the road wound through forested areas with gold, orange, and red leaves clinging to the trees. Farms dotted the landscape, with cattle, pigs, and sheep grazing between long, ancient-looking stone walls. Picturesque towns came and went, each with at least one church featuring a tall bell tower that reached toward the sky.

"I can't believe how beautiful it is!" Miranda exclaimed again, pointing at the mountains rising behind a distant valley, snow visible at the peaks, with the bluest of lakes shimmering in front of it. "The colors take my breath away."

"At this time of year, you won't see all the flowers that Spaniards like to grow everywhere but, yes. The fall color and green valleys are still pretty. Have you not been to Spain before?"

"No. I haven't been to Europe at all."

"What?" Stunned eyes flicked her way before he returned them to the curving road in front of them. "How is that possible? Surely the Davenports travel all over the world."

Miranda struggled with how much to say about her life, explaining when and how she'd come to live with the Davenports, but decided to settle on a basic answer. Going into the strange, sad, and upsetting truth of her past, and the rest of her family's, would put a damper on the drive she was enjoying more than she could remember enjoying anything in a long time.

"Well, I was in college, then medical school, which takes a lot of time and focus, you know? Then I went on a few medical missions to Africa and Central America before working at Manhattan Mercy. I do go on vacation but they tend to be short breaks."

"I respect the single-minded focus and dedication it takes to become a doctor. And that you worked on medical missions says good things about you, Miranda."

The admiring smile he gave her made her tummy get squishy and she could feel herself blush. "Not really. Just another way to use the skills I'd learned." And to hone them more in a place where the Davenport reputation wouldn't hang over everything she did, making her nervous that she might let the whole family down if she made some mistake. Which probably meant that working overseas had been more selfish than altruistic.

"So." She moved the subject to him, because she'd wondered a lot about who he really was since the moment they'd met. "Did you ever think about going to medical school?"

"Honestly? Yes. For just a short time." His

voice held an odd tone—a smile tinged with maybe bitterness? "Since I planned to leave Spain, my parents would have appreciated that occupation much more. Something better to tell friends and family about why I was going to the U.S. I realized, though, that while I like the medical aspect of my job, my time in the army showed me that search and rescue is in my blood. Which they never understood. But I came to see that I had to live my life for me, not for them."

She could tell that figuring that out had been a major struggle for him, and part of why she was on this trip to begin with. "Lots of people never find their calling. It's wonderful that you found yours."

"It is. And I thank you for helping me keep living my life as I want to. At least, as much as that will be possible. And now we are finally here. Welcome to the Castillo de Adelaide Fernanda."

A keypad was imbedded in a tall stone wall that seemed to surround the entire front of the property, and Mateo leaned out his window to punch in some numbers. Ornate iron gates probably ten feet high slowly swung inward as Mateo nosed the car through, then up a sloping, curved driveway, and Miranda couldn't contain a gasp at what lay at the top of the hill.

A huge, obviously very old stone house with a terracotta tiled roof sat nestled on lush green grass, looking nearly as though it was a natural part of the landscape. Other buildings made of stone or wood in various sizes could be seen not too far away, some surrounded by trees and others completely stark. Forests and fields seemed to stretch forever, with long stone walls dividing the spaces, and Miranda turned to stare at Mateo.

"Is…is all this your family's? It looks like it goes on for miles!"

"The estate is about one hundred and twenty-five hectares, which translates to about three hundred acres. We have livestock, farmland, and an equestrian center where show horses are bred and sometimes shown. The horses were always a big part of my and Emilio's lives when we were growing up, but when my father became too ill to manage the estate, they became my brother's passion. I…don't know what's going to happen with that part of the business now that he's not here to run it anymore. It's one of the things I'll have to talk with my parents about."

She looked at his profile, unable to read his impassive expression. "A lot of things to figure out, I'm sure. I'm sorry this is going to be a difficult trip for you."

He didn't respond, and she had to wonder if the mere act of driving through those iron gates had brought home to him full force the challenges he'd have to deal with on this visit. Since he didn't seem to want to go into that right now, Miranda made small talk about the amazing views until he stopped the car in a wide, circular turnaround in front of the house.

"We'll go inside and see where my mother has decided to put her house guest. I didn't tell her who my guest was—we get to surprise everyone."

"You didn't warn your parents ahead of time that it's the woman from your apartment, and that we're...er...engaged?"

"What was the point of having them stew about it in advance and be ready with protests? The military tactic of surprising the enemy is always a good strategy."

"Your parents aren't the enemy, Mateo. Remember that they've had a hard time of it recently, too."

"Believe me, I remind myself of that every day. And, no, not the enemy, but hostile to my chosen way of life? Yes." He turned his dark, shadowed eyes to her as they walked up stone steps to the massive arched wooden door decorated with a large, evergreen wreath with pine cones and a red bow. "But I know they don't understand, and are dealing with their own struggles. I plan to tread lightly, I promise."

Mateo swung open the huge door, and the moment they stepped inside, a plump, friendly woman came rushing up, exclaiming in Spanish as she wrapped her arms around him in a big hug.

"*Hola*, Paula! It's good to see you." Smiling, he hugged her back, and Miranda was struck by the joyous way he was being greeted by this woman compared to his mother's interactions with him in his apartment in New York. "I'd like you to meet Dr. Miranda Davenport. Miranda doesn't speak Spanish, so we'll stick to English, hmm?"

"*Sí, sí!* It is very nice to meet you, Dr. Davenport. Please come in." To Miranda's astonishment, Paula gave her a quick, motherly hug, too, and she wasn't sure what to do, finally giving her a hesitant hug back. Another stark contrast. Vanessa Davenport hadn't hugged her in her life, and being embraced by this woman felt uncomfortable yet oddly nice at the same time, bringing back long-ago memories of her own mother's love. "The guest house is all ready for you. Alfonso will get your luggage."

"Thank you. What I've seen of the place so far is beautiful, and I'm looking forward to my visit."

"Mr. Mateo will show you around as soon as you're settled. I have some breakfast waiting for you—after your long trip through the night, you must be hungry, *sí*?"

Right on cue, Miranda's stomach growled.

"Oh, dear!" The way Paula chuckled kept her from feeling bad about that. "I didn't even know I was hungry until you mentioned it. Thank you."

She glanced at Mateo's face, and was surprised to see a scowl there, which made her flush scarlet. Had she embarrassed him?

"Paula, I don't want you to call me Mr. Mateo. You've called me Mateo my whole life."

"I must!" Paula looked shocked. "You are the heir now! You are owed that respect."

"But…" Mateo looked like he wanted to keep arguing, but sighed instead. "All right. Are Mother and Father having breakfast?"

"No. They left for a doctor appointment in Barcelona. I expect them to be gone most of the day but back to dine with you tonight."

Miranda's core relaxed a little at this news. She hadn't even realized her belly had been tensely knotted about meeting Mateo's parents, and how they'd react to their "news." Based on what she'd seen so far, and what Mateo had said, it wouldn't be with happy, open arms, the way Paula had greeted them. But she was here to support him, right? Help him smooth the way with his family as they all moved into a new reality now that their son and brother was dead.

"Isn't Barcelona pretty far?" Miranda asked in a low tone as they were ushered back to the kitchen. "Your dad doesn't have a doctor that's close by?"

"The local doctor practiced for years, and didn't retire until he was well into his seventies. But now we have no one, and even though Barcelona is only about an hour away, it isn't very convenient for all the people who live and work on the various estates around here."

The kitchen was huge; ancient and modern at the same time. Arched stone walls and doorways met intricately tiled floors, and the cabinetry was a dark cherry wood. A cheerful fire in a large stone fireplace at one end warmed the space, as did homey touches like copper pans on the walls, a verdigris teakettle on the big, modern stove, and colorful plates and cups lined across a large wooden hutch.

"Sit, sit. I have made all your favorites, Mr. Mateo."

His lips twisted as he shook his head, guiding them to sit at the long table while Paula moved to the stove. "How am I going to get her to stop calling me that?"

"If I had to guess, you're not. Just go with it. If you're not home all that often, it'll just be here in Spain that you are 'Mr. Mateo.' Unless you'd like me to tell the other EMTs and staff at the hospital to use it when speaking to you."

"Funny."

His tight lips relaxed into a small smile, and she was glad she'd made the joke. She gazed around at the large expanse of the kitchen, awed at how beautiful and comfortable it was. "Your home is incredible, Mateo. And I know I've barely seen any of it yet."

"It is beautiful. I admit I've taken its beauty for granted all my life. It feels strange to be here without Emilio, though. He and I wreaked a lot of havoc in this room, and the whole house, over the years."

He stared out the wide window overlooking pastureland, and Miranda's heart squeezed at the pain etched on his face. "I know how that feels. But over time the memories become ones that make you smile more than those that bring you pain."

"I know."

He turned back to her and reached for her hand, and she gave it a little squeeze before she realized he'd doubtless been giving Paula hints about their "relationship." She tugged it loose to tuck both hands in her lap. "Why is the house called the Castillo de Adelaide Fernanda?"

"Named after a great-great-, however many greats, grandmother. I'll give you a full tour after you've rested, since I know you didn't get much sleep on the plane."

"I admit I'm a little sleepy." The words sent a

sudden, deep fatigue through her bones, and had her covering an unexpected yawn, which made Mateo chuckle. "Oh, dear. I'm sorry. But you put that idea in my head."

"And once you have a good meal by Paula in your stomach, you will need a nap for sure. Then when you're feeling energetic again? A little adventuring this afternoon. If you'll join me, Miranda?"

His dark, brooding eyes met hers. The man who'd seemed like he wanted nothing more than a fun adventure with her was gone, replaced by this grim-looking stranger, and her stomach bunched in knots at the reality of the situation.

Mateo was dealing with grief over the loss of his beloved brother. Also his parents' lack of appreciation and their expectations, along with those of everyone who worked here. All that was tangled up with the life he'd made for himself in New York. She understood well those kinds of awful and overwhelming feelings, and how they could affect every aspect of your life if you let them.

Then there was Paula, obviously delighted over their engagement and Mateo being the heir now, having no idea he didn't want to be, or that their relationship wasn't real. When Miranda had agreed to the fake engagement, it had seemed like such a harmless thing. Something to tell his parents to help him smooth over his wanting to stay mostly in New York. But seeing Paula's happiness drove a nasty pang of guilt straight into Miranda's gut.

Was this charade really a huge mistake, and had she done more harm than good by agreeing to it?

CHAPTER FIVE

MATEO PAUSED ON his way to the guest house, which was perched on a part of the property that overlooked the valley, below where the estate's sheep roamed. He breathed in the brisk November air and stared across the golden pastures, memories of his childhood flooding his mind and heart. Good memories of times spent with his brother, with the animals and the horses. Not so good memories of his parents always putting Emilio first, pandering to his every need as the future Duke, even when he hadn't wanted them to.

Now that he was here, he was filled with confusion about exactly what his mission needed to be.

He knew that living here full-time was the last thing he wanted to do. Flooded with constant reminders that his brother would never be here again. Being a disappointment to his parents, where they expected things from him he couldn't give. Accepting a bride of their choice, complete with providing grandchildren, which was never going to happen.

Being married at all had never been on his list of life goals. The girls and women of his youth here in Catalonia, and at college, had all seemed to care about the same things his sister-in-law cared about. Money and prestige and titles and power, and who would want to be saddled with that kind of woman? A fate worse than death, as far as he was concerned.

Or, maybe, a fate that led to one's death.

The thought made Mateo's chest ache. When he'd agreed to his brother's pleas to keep the kind of woman he was married to a secret from their parents, he'd had no idea what he was promising. That the burden of a secret like that could lead to terrible consequences.

He rubbed his hands over his eyes. Tried to remind himself that he didn't know for sure if that's why his brother had become more and more reckless. Regardless, he should have been here for him. Supported him and advised him, instead of living his life hiding far away in New York, where he could turn a blind eye to how bad things had gotten.

The same with his father's illness. Showing up once every couple of years hadn't been much help with his father's ongoing deterioration, but his excuse was that he'd known Emilio had been all the support they needed.

So, now they wanted to believe Mateo was good enough to take Emilio's place, when it had always been more than clear he never had been? Never would be?

No. There was a better solution that would be right for everyone, including his parents. He just had to figure out exactly what that was.

The depressing thoughts clouded his mind and threatened to put a damper on the afternoon he wanted to enjoy with Miranda. Why Emilio had loved the woman their parents had chosen for him, Mateo had no clue. Even more now that he'd met a woman like Miranda Davenport. Growing up privileged hadn't spoiled her—if anything, it must have been part of what had molded her into the strong, driven woman she was today. In fact, Miranda was the kind of woman who might change even the most hardened bachelor's mind when it came to ideas on marriage.

The thought startled him, and he wondered why his mind insisted on going to strange places. Must be from the stress of being home again, and he shook the discomfort from his shoulders to walk up the few stone steps and knock on the door.

No answer. He glanced at his watch to be sure it was 2 p.m., which was the time they'd agreed on. About to knock a second time, the door swung open with a sleepy-looking Miranda standing there in a robe, looking embarrassed.

"*Buenas tardes*, Dr. Davenport."

"Oh, I'm so sorry!" She ran her fingers through mussed brown hair. "I was so sound asleep I must have slept through my alarm. Come in."

She opened the door wider, and every uneasy thought Mateo had had moments ago evaporated. As his gaze touched her soft-looking hair, her full lips and slumberous eyes, all he could think about was the same thing that had filled his brain—and body—the last time he'd seen her wearing a robe. Thoughts of reaching for her and tangling his own fingers in her hair, of kissing that tempting mouth and sliding off that robe to touch her soft skin and see where it all might lead.

He forced his attention to the window, and cleared his throat. "We don't have to go out this afternoon if you're too tired."

Maybe that was a better plan. Keeping his distance for now probably made sense, since he'd been having trouble thinking of her as just a friend. A woman who was helping him out with a problem, someone to enjoy spending time with as he showed her the country of his birth.

Not a woman to have mind-blowing sex with,

a tempting thought that kept appearing foremost in his mind whenever he saw her, despite telling himself he shouldn't be thinking about her that way. Not when she was his guest, and had agreed to a friendly trip, not a quick affair.

"No, I'm ready. I slept well, obviously." Her lips curved in a sweet smile. "Give me five minutes to get dressed."

It felt impossible to not watch her run up the stone steps, her slender, shapely legs and bare feet making her seem very much like any other woman, and not the skilled and accomplished doctor she was.

No, not like any other woman. Something about her attracted him, drew him in, in a way he couldn't remember happening before. Minutes ticked by as he was trying to figure out exactly why, when she trotted down again to sit on the bottom step and shove on walking boots.

"This house is like a small version of your big house. So old, yet so warm and inviting. I can't believe even this space is all decorated for Christmas."

Mateo looked around at the evergreen boughs and gold ribbon wrapping the bannister, the candles circled with greenery and pinecones, the Christmas tree in the corner covered in gilded balls, and breathed in the scent. Memories from his childhood rushed back, and he was glad all of them were pleasant ones.

"My mother loves to decorate for Christmas. Has for as long as I can remember. She's often had numerous holiday parties and church gatherings, too, which the priest always appreciates. Even winter barn parties with friends in the horse business. Christmas is always a big thing at the Castillo de Adelaide Fernanda."

Miranda didn't answer, seeming to fiercely concentrate on lacing her boots, which made him wonder about Christmas at the Davenport house. "What about your family? Is Christmas a big deal?"

"Depends on who you ask, I suppose." That seemed like an odd answer, but before he could ask her what she meant, she stood and ran her hand along the stone wall. "Tell me about this guest house. Is it the same age as the main one?"

"Yes. About three hundred years old, give or take a few."

"It must be something special to not only be a part of that, but to be a member of the nobility."

"Special? I think you already know how I feel about my family obligations, Miranda." He didn't want to talk about that right now. About the deep pain and guilt he felt over Emilio's death. The reality that he wasn't the man his brother had been. The man his parents had always trusted to be there. "Is your coat in the closet? I'd like to get going so we have all afternoon before we have to be back. I suggest we take today for one of your must-sees while you're here—the sacred mountain of Montserrat. What do you think?"

"I think I'm up for anything you suggest." Finally, he got a smile, which managed to make him smile, too. "Especially since I didn't have time to grab a travel guide and research what all you have to see and do here in Catalonia, and have no idea what Montserrat is."

"You have a travel guide, and that is me."

"Which makes me very lucky, I'm sure."

"I believe I'm the lucky one to get to show you around." He helped her slip on her coat, knowing that was beyond true. "I hope you'll be impressed and amazed by what we're going to see, Dr. Davenport."

"Those words fill me with breathless anticipation, Mr. Alves."

Twinkling blue eyes had his hand sliding down her arm to grasp her hand, because it just felt right. "Then let's get going."

The ride in the car was filled with conversation about the places they passed, and at other times a silence so comfortable it struck him as unusual for two people who didn't really know one another.

For probably the twentieth time, Mateo turned

to look at the woman sitting in the passenger seat, anticipation welling in his chest at what her reaction might be to seeing Monserrat. He still remembered the first time his nanny had brought him and Emilio to this place. They'd been amazed by the soaring rocky crags and the thrill of riding the cable car up to see the amazing monastery nestled in the stone, looking almost as though it had simply grown there.

"Those mountains are incredible!" Miranda exclaimed, staring upward as he parked, then came around to her side to open her door. "I can't believe the shape of the stone, almost like a giant hand dribbled wet sand into spires, and they all stuck together that way."

"Wet sand fused into a mountain. I like that description—very apt. Just wait until you see how we're going to get up the mountain to see the basilica." He reached for her hand because he'd enjoyed holding it the first time, and why not? This trip might have a serious agenda, but he fully planned to enjoy the company of this smart and beautiful woman who had been surprising him since he'd first asked for her help. Since the moment she'd run into that tunnel.

"I hope it's not rappelling, like my sister Penny does. I'd probably faint, then fall to my death."

"No rappelling, promise. And falling to one's death only happens here maybe once a month."

She playfully swatted his arm and he started to laugh. With her hand tucked into the crook of his elbow, he found himself unable to keep from glancing into her smiling eyes as they moved toward the funicular.

Whenever he'd seen her in the hospital, she'd been all business, working efficiently, and not one of the docs who joked around sometimes with the staff and medics that came and went. When she'd come into that tunnel collapse, how unnerved she'd been afterward had surprised him, though it shouldn't have. Most people would be freaked out to have rubble falling on their heads, but, then, most people wouldn't have run in like that either. Angry as he'd been at her, and, yes, worried about her, he had to admire that she'd come to help even though he now knew she'd been scared the whole time. She didn't strike him as an act first, think later kind of person, so he had to assume she'd decided she had to go in there regardless of the risk, and that impressed the hell out of him, though he wasn't about to admit that to her.

"We're going to take the—"

He quit talking because she'd stopped dead, yanking him to a halt as she did. "Please don't tell me we're going to get in that yellow thing and go up into the sky."

"Well, we're not going up into the sky, we're

going to see the basilica and museum at the monastery up there, and the Black Virgin of Montserrat. But, yes, we're getting in the funicular to do that."

"Oh, my gosh." The blue eyes staring up at him were no longer smiling, they looked beyond worried. Even panicked. "I don't know. I'm sorry, Mateo, but I don't know. I never thought I had a fear of heights, but looking at that thing now has me freaking out."

"Miranda." He turned her to him and tugged her close against him. "I would never suggest you do something that frightens you. So of course we may just stay down here, and go somewhere else if you want. But if you can face your fear the way you did in the subway tunnel, I can promise you that seeing the basilica, the Black Virgin, and the incredible views will make you glad you did."

She pressed her hands against his chest and stared at him, her eyes still wide, but looking a little less panicked now. "I'm being silly, aren't I?"

"Not silly. You know as well as I do that lots of people have a fear of heights. But I can tell you that I'm an expert at that rappelling you don't want to do. So if the cable car gets stuck, I'll hold you in my arms like Tarzan with Jane, and we'll still make it down."

She managed a weak laugh. "I can't say that really reassures me."

"It should. I really have rescued a number of people that way, whether it was on a mountainside or a building or from a helicopter while I was in the military. But the odds of having to do that fall into the slim-to-none category, as I've never heard of the cable car getting stuck. I'm as sure as I can possibly be that it's completely safe."

"All right." A steely look of determination came to her face that reminded him of how she'd looked in the tunnel when he'd told her to leave. "Let's do it. And I apologize in advance if I hyperventilate or hold on to you too tightly."

"I can handle either scenario." He hoped she didn't hyperventilate, but her holding on to him? Now, that he'd be more than fine with. "And I'll do what I can to make you feel more comfortable."

With that promise, he wrapped one arm around her shoulders while holding her hand with the other. Miranda squeezed it hard and, as the cable car jerked to a start, pinched her eyes shut. Mateo had to grin at her cutely scrunched-up face. Soon, though, her worried expression wasn't funny at all as the slight sway of the cable car and the chilly breeze touching their skin seemed to ratchet up her panic big time.

"Oh, God, Mateo. I don't think I can do this."

Looking like she might actually cry, she practically cut off the circulation in his hand as she gulped in breaths. "Damn it, Miranda. I feel terrible that this is making you miserable."

"I… I can do it."

"You can. You *are* doing it. Look upward at the clouds instead of down. I think that one looks a little like Benny, don't you? Except not as fat."

As he'd hoped, giving her something to think about besides how high they were seemed to calm her slightly. "Definitely not as fat." She sucked in a breath and pointed at another cloud formation. "That one looks a little like the beautiful Christmas tree in the guest house, doesn't it?"

That she was trying so hard to act brave and composed when she obviously didn't feel that way tugged at his heart. Just like when he'd realized later that the show of confidence and determination in the tunnel had been an act.

Miranda was the kind of woman who donned a persona of perfection, acting the way she expected others wanted and expected her to, even if it made her suffer.

"It does look a lot like a Christmas tree, doesn't it?" He grasped her chin and gently turned her face toward him, and the obvious anxiety there sent a sharp stab of guilt into his chest. "We'll be on solid ground soon, Miranda. Hang in there for just a few more minutes, okay?"

He pressed his cheek to hers, cupping her face in his hand as he held her close. "Just close your eyes. Think about wonderful, beautiful things you enjoy. What are those things?"

"Puppies and kittens," she whispered against his skin. "Babies. Snow. Walking in nature. Cake. Especially cake."

"Now you're talking." He smiled, hearing her relax a little, feeling the tenseness in her neck and arms fade. "What kind of cake?"

"Chocolate. Rich chocolate with chocolate icing, too, but really any kind of cake makes me happy."

"Good to know. It's also good that you like to walk in nature, because that's our next excursion, no scary heights involved. And see?" The funicular squeaked and jerked as it swung into the terminal, and Mateo found himself pressing a lingering kiss to her warm cheek before pulling back. "Here we are, safely on the mountain. You made it! And I think going down won't be as scary."

Her hands slowly slid from his shoulders as she opened her eyes and looked around. With a deep breath, her gaze turned to his. "I'm so sorry I was such a baby. Thank you for helping me get through it."

"You weren't a baby, you were expressing genuine fear, and we all have things we're afraid of, don't we? Believe me, I saw lots of men break down during training exercises in the military, even when they knew they weren't in real danger but were scared anyway. Human nature, right?"

"Right. Thank you for...for not judging me."

Did the woman often feel like she was being judged? He couldn't imagine that, considering her stellar reputation at the hospital. Then again, he knew first-hand what it felt like to be judged by people close to you.

He held her hand as they exited the car, and some of his guilt faded when a genuine smile lit her face as they walked along the wide path, looking at the scenery surrounding them.

"This is breathtaking! The mountains are like none I've ever seen before. And the monastery looks like it's almost part of the rock, you know?" Her grip on his hand loosened, and that blue gaze turned to his, a look of awe sliding over her face. "The engineering that had to go into that funicular is incredible. I wonder how they built it?"

"Impressive engineering, yes. But since it was done with modern equipment, to me, it's not as incredible as getting the monastery built. You said you haven't traveled in Europe so you haven't seen the many fortresses built high on mountains to keep the population safer from marauders, and make it easier to see enemies coming. You should plan to do a European tour soon. Even growing up here, I still marvel every time I see one of them."

"I had some chances to travel with my family, but knew I had to concentrate on college and medical school instead. All that didn't come as naturally to me as it did to my siblings, you know? They're all superstars in their own ways."

She seemed utterly serious, which Mateo couldn't believe. He might not know the Davenports personally, but being around Miranda for mere hours showed she wasn't just smart, she had street-smarts and people-smarts that not everyone with a high IQ possessed.

"I might not know you well, Miranda, but you seem like a superstar to me."

Her face turned pink and she gave him a shy smile. "Thanks, but you obviously don't know my siblings very well. And wasn't I just about to have a panic attack on the way up here?"

"Irrelevant to being a superstar. And even though you were scared, you handled it just fine."

"I think it's because you made me feel safer. Just like in the tunnel. So thank you for that. Sometimes…well, there have been a few times in my life when feeling safe was hard to come by."

The almost shy look of gratitude on her face

bothered him. What had he done for her other than hold her close and tell her it would be okay? What exactly did she mean by not feeling safe at times? Did no one she knew support her?

"No thanks necessary." His voice came out a little gruff. "I'm glad I could help. So now that we're here, I can't wait for you to see why you made the effort."

The tour of the basilica and museum seemed to fascinate Miranda, and her pleasure at seeing them made him smile too. How long had it been since he'd been up here? Too long, as his parents had pointed out, and the now familiar guilt of all that pressed on his chest.

He shook off those thoughts, wanting to enjoy being alone with Miranda for the short time he had. "Quite a few monks still live here at the Montserrat Abbey, though I doubt if we'll see them. And right over here is the Black Virgin. One story says she was brought here during an eighth-century invasion for protection. She lay in hiding until being rediscovered about two hundred years later. Today, many people come to pay homage to her."

"Oh, she's so beautiful!" Miranda breathed as she looked at the statue. "I've never seen anything like this. What is she made of?"

"It's said she was carved from wood in Jerusalem. Apparently her dark color is from hundreds of years of candles being burned in front of her, though she has been painted black more than once over the centuries. Many have reported miracles after being here."

"There was a time I didn't believe in miracles, but then one happened to me. And this place is so amazing, who knows?"

"Indeed. Who knows?" Personally, Mateo didn't believe in miracles, though he'd never tell his deeply Catholic mother that. "What miracle happened to you?"

Her smile grew a little stiff. "Not important. Silly of me to say that, really. It wasn't really a miracle. So now where do we go?"

"It's possible to climb to the cave where the Black Virgin was hidden, but that's very strenuous. We should probably just explore the area a little more then head back, to give you time to rest before having to pretend to be my adoring fiancée."

"Adoring? I don't remember that being part of our deal."

"Ah, my mother may get frustrated with me, but I think she'd expect my fiancée to think I'm wonderful."

She chuckled, obviously knowing he was teasing. But, truthfully, he was a little worried how his parents would react to his pretend engagement. Being surprised and not happy that she was an American was a given. But would they be cool with her, or possibly rude? They certainly hadn't been very cordial to her at his apartment.

His parents were normally polite, but the loss of their beloved elder son had hit them both hard. He knew they were still grieving deeply, and worried about his father's health. Weren't they all? That pain and worry, combined with feeling stressed over the future of the dukedom, had taken their toll, eating away at their innate decorum.

He sighed. If only this plan with Miranda would make his parents decide they wanted him to be there only part of the time anyway. Choosing a bride—pretending to choose—who they wouldn't deem suitable for the future Duke would hopefully give them second thoughts about their insistence that he come back permanently. He might not be able to ignore the guilt gnawing at his gut, but thinking about living here full-time made his stomach churn.

No point in fighting that argument with himself all over again. The week with Miranda here posing as his fiancée would unfold as it would, and he'd figure out the next steps as they went along.

Thankfully, their trip down the funicular didn't seem to stress Miranda as much as coming up had, and they talked like old friends on the drive back. Mateo was struck all over again at the odd connection he felt with her. Maybe it had something to do with the ruse, but he didn't think so. He'd felt that way during the very first hours they'd spent together during and after the tunnel collapse. A mysterious chemistry that just happened sometimes, he supposed, but he couldn't remember feeling so utterly relaxed and happy to be with someone, even as the dreaded first meeting with his parents loomed over them.

"Here we are, with plenty of time for you to rest before dinner." He drove straight up to the guest house. "Thank you for joining me, and for not hating me for putting you through the funicular."

"It's good for me to face my fears. Maybe that's the big lesson I'm going to get from this trip."

"I hope it won't be full of fears for you to over-come, Miranda. That it will be more about ad-venture and having fun together." The truth of that struck him as he remembered how scared and vulnerable she'd looked, and how protective it had made him feel. As much as he wanted her here to help him with his family problems, he knew that, even more, he wanted to help her feel more confident and appreciated, which seemed to be lacking in her life for some inexplicable reason.

With that goal now forefront in his mind, he nudged her into the guest house, slipped off her coat, and pressed a kiss to her forehead, wishing he could kiss her for real. "Get some rest. I'll be back at seven to take you to the house."

"Okay."

That uncomfortable look slipped onto her face again, and it made his chest tighten. He knew then that he had to somehow try to smooth the rough edges off the meeting with his parents ahead of time. Let them know they had to be on their best behavior without actually telling them about the engagement, because he had a feeling that if they had too much time to think about it before they met her, they'd be so upset they'd forget their manners entirely.

"They're not ogres, Miranda. It will be fine, I promise."

"I know. I'm being silly. Again. It's not even a real engagement, anyway, so there's no reason them being upset should bother me."

"Right. See you in a bit." He gave her a smile and a quick hug to hopefully reassure her before heading to the house to find his parents.

"Paula. Are Mother and Father here?"

"They got back from the doctor's about an hour ago, and are having coffee in the front room."

Seeing them sitting like they always did in

their favorite chairs made him feel a warm familiarity, at the same time the knife edge of guilt stabbed his gut. His mother was reading, but his father just stared out the window.

Something about seeing them here at home was different than when they'd been in New York, and the knife twisted deeper. How had he not noticed how thin his father had gotten? How pallid and frail? Even his hair, which had always been thick and difficult to tame, seemed thinner and more gray. But grief as well as illness could age a person, and it struck him that both his parents looked about ten years older than they had at his brother's funeral.

Mateo's throat tightened, and he had to swallow before he could speak. "Madre. Padre. How did the doctor appointment go?"

"Mateo!" His mother stood and wrapped her arms around him and he held her close for a long moment, trying to remember the last time he'd done that. "Paula told us you and your friend were here, and had gone out for a bit."

"Yes, we went to Montserrat. I haven't been there for a long time."

"You haven't been home at all for a long time, other than for your brother's funeral."

And here they were, straight to familiar criticism. He bit back a negative response, instead walking to his father's chair and crouching down to grasp his bony hands. "How are you feeling?"

"Not bad."

Mateo knew his father's pride demanded that he be stoic, and he was never sure how to handle that. Whether or not he should leave it at that, or ask specific questions about his father's difficulty sleeping, or if his co-ordination was worsening, or if he was scared at the ways his body functions were deteriorating.

"Any new medications or therapies they want to try?"

"They want him to try a new medicine for his tremor, and see if it will also help him walk better," his mother answered.

Mateo nodded, making a mental note to look later at what they'd given him. He gently squeezed his father's hands, then stood. "Well, as you know, my…friend is here with me. Thank you, Madre, for having the guest house looking so beautiful. Your special Christmas touches are everywhere, which Miranda appreciates."

A smile banished the seriousness and disapproval he'd come to expect from her. "I'm glad. What time are you bringing her here?"

"Paula told me seven. Is that right?"

"Yes. We look forward to it. But remember, Mateo."

Her stern expression back, he had a feeling he knew what was coming. "Remember what?"

"We have important things to talk about privately. So be sure to leave us with plenty of time to do that before you go back to the States."

He glanced at his father, who was just looking at him with those scarily sunken eyes. When he turned back to his frowning mother, his gut tightened as he realized all over again how complicated this situation really was. How hard it was going to be to find a solution that made everyone reasonably happy. "I won't forget. And I hope that, despite that upcoming conversation, you'll be cordial and welcoming to Miranda. See you in a few hours."

CHAPTER SIX

MIRANDA CURLED HER fingers into her palms, the ring on her finger feeling strangely uncomfortable. She stared at the huge, heavy wood front door of Mateo's family home, awed by it all over again. Small evergreen trees covered with twinkling lights sat in decorative concrete pots that at each side of the wide stone porch, and the whole house looked like something out of a travel magazine during the holidays.

The door opened before they reached it, with Paula standing there, all smiles. "Welcome! Come in! Your parents are expecting you in the blue salon for drinks and appetizers before dinner."

"Thanks, Paula." Mateo took Miranda's hand and thumbed the ring as they walked into his parents' house. The feel of his hand holding hers might have eased her discomfort about their upcoming big "announcement" to his parents if he hadn't been wearing a slightly grim expression. "Thank you for wearing this. I appreciate it."

And how strange had it felt slipping it on? It wasn't as though she'd ever been in a school play to hone the minimum of acting skills required for this charade. At the same time, though, she couldn't deny that wearing such a gorgeous ring would be nice under different circumstances. Like a real engagement to someone she loved, and thinking about this deception had her feeling nervous and uncomfortable all over again. Was it wrong of her—and of Mateo—to be deceiving his parents this way?

Butterflies flapped around in Miranda's belly, even though she knew it didn't make sense, since she'd known all along why she was on this trip in the first place. And she'd already met Mateo's parents, right? Or sort of met them. While wearing Mateo's robe. With him naked in the other room.

Heat flooded her cheeks to join her nervous jitters. It seemed only a few hours ago she'd been so happy she'd agreed to come to Spain with Mateo. Now? Now she knew that *crazy* was exactly that—what had she been thinking?

"Are you ready?"

"I'm… Honestly, I don't know." She looked around the amazing old house, with its stone walls, fine carpets, and gorgeous furniture. Decorated even more lavishly for Christmas than the guest house, and she felt more out of place than when she'd first moved in with the Davenports as a teen. "I feel uncomfortable. I'm not sure I'll be able to act like we're engaged, to convince your parents that we really are."

"Then I'll be sure to do something to make you feel more convincing, hmm?"

She stared up into his dark eyes, filled with an impish teasing that had banished his frown. What that "something" might be had her worrying even more as he led her into a beautifully appointed room. A stunning Christmas tree so tall it touched the high ceiling was loaded with small white lights, gorgeous and unusual ornaments, and silver tinsel. Several surfaces in the room featured golden angels and heavy candles set in loops of evergreen that smelled wonderful.

The long, wide room they entered, filled with two settees and comfortable-looking chairs, was empty of humans, which had Miranda drawing a deep breath of relief. Maybe his parents weren't coming after all. The second that hope came to mind, she chided herself for the ridiculous thought. Getting together with them and making their big announcement was the whole point of the evening, and the entire trip, wasn't it?

"How about a drink? A cocktail or a glass of wine?"

"Wine, please. White." With any luck, maybe a little alcohol would calm her nerves, because right now they were jangling so much she thought Mateo might actually hear them.

He didn't let go of her hand until they'd walked to a well-stocked bar made of what looked like carved mahogany. After pouring wine into two crystal glasses, his dark gaze lifted to hers, so intense she wondered what he might be seeing on her face.

Then, to her utter shock, his hands cupped her face and he kissed her. Not a chaste kiss either—it was a full onslaught of heat that stole her breath and ignited a flame deep inside her quivering belly. The light scent of his cologne filled her nose and a tingle swept from her head to her toes as they curled in her shoes. The surprise of it faded as quickly as the kiss had begun, his mouth moving on hers so slowly, so expertly her heart pounded hard as she leaned into him. Her hands lifted to his wide shoulders and her head tipped involuntarily to one side, wanting more of the hot, delicious taste of him.

Just as she was sinking so deeply into the kiss she felt dizzy from it, he lifted his head. Barely able to open her eyes, she met his heated gaze, dark and alive, only to see it slide right past her one second later.

"Ah, Madre. Padre. I'm sorry, I didn't see you come in," Mateo said smoothly, not seeming at all embarrassed.

Dazed, Miranda spun to see his parents standing just inside the room, and horror froze her veins. First they'd seen her fresh from the shower, then kissing Mateo like she wanted to devour him whole. She was positive that's what it had looked like, because that's exactly how she'd felt. Good Lord, they probably thought she was a sex addict or something.

For a wild second, she wondered if that might be true, considering her embarrassing reaction to Mateo's kiss.

His parents both stood motionless, staring. Then with deep frowns they slowly moved toward the two settees set across from one another. A coffee table was placed between the couches, and Paula was currently putting plates on it, piled high with several kinds of food.

"You told us you were bringing a guest. We thought it was one of your old friends from here." And it was more than obvious that his mother was not at all pleased that it wasn't.

"Why would you assume that?"

"Because of our new situation. Your obligations."

Mateo didn't respond to that comment, but she could see him working to seem relaxed. Miranda tried hard to shore up indifference, remind herself she was here to help Mateo and not win a popularity contest, but couldn't help but feel that familiar hollow in her gut. The one she'd felt when she'd first shown up at the Davenport home to face Vanessa Davenport's hostility. That she felt every time she was at a family event she was supposed to pretend to be a part of, despite Vanessa's dislike.

"I don't see what our…difficulties have to do with Miranda. And I wanted it to be a surprise." He cupped Miranda's waist as he turned to her with an adoring smile on his face so convincing it was startling. The man should receive an acting award. "I was horribly amiss in not introducing you the last time you met. Miranda, I'd like you to meet my parents, Rafael and Ana. Mother and Father, I'd like you to meet my fiancée, Dr. Miranda Davenport."

"Fiancée?" Ana sank into the sofa, her face blanching so much that Miranda worried she might faint. "What?"

"I know this comes as a shock." Mateo tugged her closer. She wondered if he'd sensed that her legs felt a little wobbly, and she definitely needed the support. "Miranda and I met at a tunnel collapse, rescuing a man together. And it was love at first sight, wasn't it, *querida*?"

His smile was wide and coaxing, and she wanted to say, *Not exactly. I believe you yelled and cursed at me.* But she'd come here to help Mateo, though the way his mother was looking at her, like an unwelcome rodent that had found its way into their home, made her suddenly wish with all her heart that she'd never agreed to this.

"Yes, Mateo is a very special man." She choked out the words, though they should have been easy to say since she knew it was true. Giving him the adoring gaze he was giving her might be even harder, but she tried, forcing her lips to curve into a stiff smile. "He swept me off my feet. Literally."

Mateo chuckled and pressed his mouth to her temple, sliding it to her ear. "Nicely done," he whispered. "Thank you for letting me kiss you."

Her chest deflated a little, and she instantly berated herself for feeling disappointed at his words. Hadn't she realized almost immediately that he'd only kissed her because they had an audience? Why would it hurt her feelings to hear him confirm it?

"I can't believe you didn't discuss this with us first." His father focused his attention on Mateo as though Miranda wasn't even there. "If you had stayed here, where you belong, we wouldn't be so distant from one another. Why you had to move to New York is still a mystery to us. And to be an EMT when you could have chosen a dozen other careers here in Spain!"

"I chose to be an EMT because that's the path that called to me. As did New York City. I could be anyone there, not treated differently because of who I am. Surely you understand that."

"Yet you are part of this family, whether you like it or not. You must take on your responsibilities now that you are the heir." His father's voice quavered. "And marriage is a big decision. We would have liked to participate in that."

"I understand that." Miranda could see he was taking time to choose his words carefully. "I know Emilio was comfortable with you deciding who he should marry. But I'm a grown man who wants to decide on my own if, who, and when I'll marry."

"Camilla is a lovely girl, Mateo, and Emilio was very happy with her," Ana protested. "You would do well to have a bride as lovely a person as she is. You have a responsibility to marry someone who understands our culture. Who is one of us."

Miranda's gut clenched at their total dismissal of her. Even though their engagement was fake, she couldn't deny it felt horrible to be an interloper yet again. Someone utterly unwelcome to the matriarch of the house. Hadn't she spent years trying to come to terms with that? Being faced with it again, however temporarily, made her want to run from the room and never come back.

Maybe Mateo sensed she was about to flee because his grip on her tightened. His jaw ticked and he seemed to take a moment to draw breath before he spoke again. "I do have a bride who is not only a lovely person, she's a physician as well. I would appreciate it if you would welcome her—the first woman I have ever brought here."

"You should have warned us," Ana said sharply. "An American is not a suitable bride for you, as you well know."

"Perhaps in your view," Mateo said in a remarkably calm voice, considering the twitch Miranda could see in his jaw. "But I believe that the people who live here would welcome a beautiful, intelligent and accomplished woman as their duchess, don't you?"

Miranda stared up at him, wondering how he managed to sound so relaxed when his parents were attacking him. She also wondered about the glib compliments falling from his lips. Had she ever been called those things by anyone?

"The people who live here value our long heritage, Mateo. Something an outsider would not understand," Rafael said.

"You are being very selfish here, Mateo." Ana narrowed her eyes at him before sliding them toward Miranda. "An unwelcome shock like this is not good for your father's health. What is so hard about accepting your duties here? Your brother never hesitated to take on the role when asked.

And yet you act like it's a burden to even come home briefly to visit."

"I'm fully aware of Father's health, and my duties. The pain we all feel over losing Emilio. I'm sorry to be such a grave disappointment to both of you."

"You are not a disappointment, Mateo." Frowning, his mother waved her hand. "It's just that…we are having a party here tomorrow to celebrate your coming home. I would prefer not to announce this…engagement yet. Give you some time to think more about it."

"There's nothing to think about." Mateo's voice had become hard now, and the look he was giving them would have had most people quaking in their shoes. "Miranda and I are engaged to be married, which I want announced to the world. In addition to that, I would appreciate some civility and manners toward her, which so far have been sorely lacking from you."

His parents glanced at one another, each huffing out a frustrated breath as they seemed to realize how unpleasant they'd been. "Our apologies, Dr. Davenport. This is…a very big surprise, but we certainly want all our guests to feel welcome here. Please sit down and have something to eat."

The thought of trying to swallow anything make Miranda choke. They wanted her to feel welcome? That wasn't going to happen because to say she was most definitely *not* welcome would be an understatement. And the way they spoke to Mateo? Anger on his behalf tightened her chest. She knew all too well how it felt to be talked to as though you're an outsider by someone who was supposedly family. If she didn't get out of there, she might say something she'd regret.

"Please call me Miranda," she said, drawing in a calming breath. "It's very nice to meet you. But I'm afraid I can't stay to eat at the moment. The…the busy day and traveling has left me feeling a little unwell. I'm sorry, but I'll have to visit with you a little later. Excuse me."

She pulled from Mateo's grasp and practically ran from the room. It wasn't a lie that she didn't feel well. Her stomach roiled as she hurried through the huge French doors at the back of the house that opened to a patio, and beyond to a garden that even in November was appealing.

The brisk air felt wonderful on her hot cheeks, and she gratefully gulped in large breaths of it. The moon hanging above the carefully trimmed hedges and shrubs lining the stone paths was barely larger than a sliver, but it cast enough light for her to see where she was going.

She'd wanted an adventure. Wanted to see more of Spain. Wanted to spend a little time with interesting and attractive Mateo Alves. But not anymore. Not when they'd said loud and clear how they felt about her being there.

Maybe she should just go home. Or somewhere else. Get on a train to Italy or France, or a plane to somewhere warm, before going back to cold and gray New York. Avoiding Thanksgiving with her family so she didn't have to feel like an outsider hadn't worked out so well, had it? She'd ended up feeling exactly the same way, worse even, in someone else's home.

Mateo could find some other solution to his problems with his family. She felt bad for him—she did. But she'd done what she'd promised, right? She'd posed as his fiancée, and now she could leave if she wanted to. Maybe he could still leverage that into the extra time he wanted to let his parents know he wasn't moving back permanently, and, wow, she sure understood now why he didn't want to.

A shiver racked her, and she wrapped her arms around herself, realizing she'd been in such a hurry to get away from the smothering situation in the house that she hadn't grabbed her coat. About to turn back, she felt warm wool drape over her shoulders and big hands holding it there. She didn't have to turn to know it was her own coat and Mateo's hands.

"I'm so sorry, Miranda." His fierce voice rumbled in her ear. "I knew they wouldn't be happy, but their behavior was worse than I expected. I apologize for the way they acted."

"It's okay."

"No, it's not okay. I'm trying to excuse them because they're frustrated with me that I moved away, now leaving our estate without anyone to manage it full-time. They're worried about my father's health problems, and I admit he looks more frail than I'd realized. And they're still struggling with the pain of my brother's death, their favorite son. I hope you understand that it's all a very heavy weight on them."

"Favorite son?" Miranda stared, then realized he was utterly serious. "Why would you say that? They want you to come back to your home. To take your brother's place."

"Only because he's gone. Believe me, there was no doubt they considered their elder son to be their best son. They insisted he serve only one year in the Spanish army because they needed him here. He was always a huge support to both of them. Whereas they were happy for me to serve four years, and I'm thankful for that. It helped me find my calling, which is one of the reasons I don't want to move back here permanently."

"Is your father too ill to take on the responsibilities of the estate again for at least a little while?"

"Unfortunately, yes." He sighed, and the deep pain in his eyes was obvious. "He was diagnosed with Parkinson's six years ago. You can see he speaks and moves slowly, and suffers from a tremor. He's diabetic as well. So it made sense for him to relinquish his responsibilities to Emilio. Except they insisted he marry as soon as possible, and chose his wife for him. As they've wanted to do for me, but I have no intention of ever getting married."

"No? You told me that on the plane, but I wasn't sure you meant it." Somehow, it didn't surprise her, though. Even when he was being charming and wonderful, there was a part of him that seemed closed off. That he didn't care to share. She wondered why, and even as she did so, that part of her brain that was self-protective started whispering again. Reminding her that she didn't really know him, that he didn't do long-term relationships, and that falling for him would be the worst idea ever. "Why not?"

"Even if it had ever crossed my mind, the way women always acted when they knew my lineage made it impossible to know if they liked me or my title. And if I ever did marry someday, it certainly wouldn't be someone of my parents' choosing. My brother's marriage definitely convinced me not to."

"It wasn't good? He didn't love her?"

"He actually cared for her very much." A bitter laugh came from his lips. "But Camilla cares only for herself, what she can buy with our family's money, and spending time with the wealthy Spaniards she's met through Emilio and my parents. She enjoys the company of men greatly, and hurt my brother deeply with her numerous affairs. I never told him that I was one of her targets before I moved to New York, but he knew about plenty of others."

"That's horrible! Why do your parents think she's so wonderful, then?"

"Emilio insisted that I not tell them, to let them continue to believe that the woman they'd chosen for their son was a paragon of virtue and a devoted wife. Which was probably a mistake on my part." He stared off toward the trees before heaving a sigh. "Anyway, I don't know how they've been able to turn a blind eye to her shallowness, though I suspect it's because they don't want to know."

The Alves family didn't have as many skeletons in the closet—or out of it—as the Davenports, but they certainly had their share. Maybe every family did.

"Listen, I get why you wanted me to come, with your parents putting pressure on you to marry someone they like, and come back here when you don't want to. But now that you've introduced me as your fiancée and they were obviously unhappy about it, I think I should leave. Maybe you can use that to play into your not coming back for a while or something. You'll have to figure that out, but I just… It's too uncomfortable for me to stay."

"Is that why you practically ran from the room? I hope you know it has nothing to do with you—it's because of their grief, and their anger with me. Please don't take it personally."

Please don't take it personally. Isn't that what her father had always told her? It was hard not to take it personally, though, when you knew that, inside, someone greatly disliked you, even when they tried not to show it.

"I'm afraid that's impossible."

"Why? My parents don't even know the real you, so why would you care what they think?" The concerned brown eyes looking down at her seemed genuinely perplexed. Probably because self-confidence practically oozed from the man.

"I… Nothing." Sharing her sad, strange and shocking life history wasn't something she enjoyed doing. Lots of people in New York and elsewhere still remembered the scandal, but if they didn't, the last thing she wanted to do was talk about it.

"Miranda." His hands cupped her cheeks as they had before, reminding her of that searing kiss. "I'd like to know why you would let my parents' attitude mean anything to you."

She stared into his eyes, and the warmth and obvious caring there, so astonishingly sincere despite having known the man only a matter of days, somehow made her want to talk about it after all. Help him understand why she needed to leave, and not be angry with her about it.

"Everyone believed that the famous Davenport family was close-knit and perfect. And to some degree they are. My brothers and sister are all close to one another, and to…to Hugo and Vanessa. Until a huge scandal rocked the Davenports' world."

"What kind of scandal?"

"Me," she whispered. "I was the scandal."

"What do you mean?"

"I grew up in Chicago with a single mom. Well, I did meet Hugo a few times, then I guess he was worried that contact between us might hurt the rest of his family, and he couldn't allow that to happen. That it wouldn't be fair to his other children and wife if they knew about me, so we didn't have any more contact."

"That makes me think less of Hugo Davenport."

"I think he was in a difficult situation. He'd made a mistake having an affair with my mother, with me as the result. He had to put his wife and family first."

"And his reputation. I think you're giving him too much credit, Miranda."

Maybe. She'd chosen not to judge him, perhaps because her mother had always insisted she shouldn't. Had told her he was a good man, and that she was the one who insisted his responsibilities were to his other family.

"So what happened?"

"My mother died when I was sixteen, and I was all alone. I didn't know what I was going to do, but she'd always shown me where her important papers were, like her will, so of course I had to go through it, to see what was there."

Talking about it felt like she'd ripped open a scab from a painful wound that still hadn't fully healed. Even thirteen years later, the memories of how horrible all that had been brought tears to her eyes. Memories of feeling so lost and alone, missing her sweet, wonderful mother, and having no idea what her future might bring other than foster homes and poverty. Filled with hopelessness and a feeling of despair, wondering if she should even make the effort to endure it.

"Ah, Miranda." His hands moved from her cheeks to her back beneath her open coat, tugging her closer against the warmth of his hard body. "What a terrible thing for you to have to go through."

She nodded, letting her forehead rest against his chest, lingering there. It felt nice, and she realized it had been a long time since she'd allowed herself to really lean on someone else.

"In her papers, I found a letter she'd written to me, telling me that if anything ever happened to her, I should contact Hugo Davenport, and she gave me his phone number and address." She lifted her gaze back to his warm one. "At first, he was shocked to hear from me. Then even more shocked when we both found out money he'd instructed his accountant give to us every month for my support had been embezzled by the guy. My mother had had no idea he'd been sending money. So I had almost no financial resources."

"What? That's unbelievable!" He stared and shook his head. "So he finally stepped up? Acknowledged you?"

"He did. I became Hugo Davenport's daughter, and a member of the Davenport family. But not before someone leaked the news, much to the media's delight and my shame."

"Your shame? Your father's shame, not yours."

"I suppose, though it didn't feel that way. The whole family was not only shocked and humiliated that their father had had an affair that was now very publicly out in the open, but that a child had been conceived as a result. I give my father credit, though. He could have just financially supported me, but instead he insisted I live with all of them. It was a little rocky at first, as you can imagine." And was that an understatement, or what? An emotional and physical upheaval for everyone in the house. "No one was sure how to deal with the person responsible for all the turmoil and embarrassment in their lives at that moment. A sister they'd never known about, a new-found daughter, a girl who was the result of your husband's infidelity."

"Dios mio," Mateo murmured. "I can't imagine. Were they unkind to you?"

"Not exactly. Distant, at first. You can guess that it felt beyond awkward, living there with all these people I didn't even know. I... I missed my mom so much." She swallowed down the tears that threatened even after all these years. "From the beginning, Charles was very kind to me. Eventually, as we spent time together, my brothers and sister accepted me, and I'm so grateful that we're close now. Especially Penny and me. Hugo went out of his way to be nice and supportive, I suppose to make up for all the years he wasn't there."

"As well he should have."

His tone was so dark and grim it made her smile a little. "I know the way he dealt with it before wasn't perfect. But his taking me in, his caring, was like a miracle. There were some dark days after my mom died, and I thought I'd be alone forever. I thought my life was over. But him wanting me to know my siblings and for them to know me was a wonderful gift. I'm coming to believe that, in spite of what I know about Hugo and Vanessa's relationship and his infidelity, good marriages do exist. That someday I might be able to find a man who loves me. A husband who will always be there for me and a family that is truly and completely my own."

"I'm surprised that you still believe that's possible, after all you've been through."

"There are a lot of times I'm not sure who I am or what I'm worth, but I'm learning as I go along."

"Now, that is something I completely understand." His gaze searched hers before he slowly nodded. "Learning things as we go along seems to be part of life, doesn't it?"

"Yeah, it does."

Thankfully, he left it at that. The insecurities she still carried around were private, and not something she liked to talk about.

Seconds ticked by before he spoke again. "You don't go into any detail about your stepmother. How did she feel about you moving in?"

"I'm sure you can guess the answer." Her lips

twisted, and her stomach did, too, because even now her resentment toward Miranda was very clear. "Vanessa hated that my father insisted I come there to live. And I get that, you know? Probably every time she looked at me, it was like a slap in her face. A reminder that her husband had cheated on her."

"Again, though, it wasn't your fault."

"She tried, I think. And I tried. I tried so hard to be a model house guest. Which is how I felt for a long time, you know? To feel like a real member of the family was impossible. No matter what I did, I was the trespasser who wasn't truly welcomed by everyone in the house. Who wasn't quite a real Davenport." She forced a smile, figuring she should just stop talking now. Knowing she had to be boring Mateo with her sad story. "Anyway. I'm sorry, but I don't want to be that unwelcome person here, too, even if it's just for a short time. Maybe that's childish of me. But I think it's best if I just go somewhere else for the rest of my vacation, and not make your parents miserable."

CHAPTER SEVEN

THE VULNERABILITY, THE little-girl-lost look he'd glimpsed back in the tunnel and again on the funicular was clear in Miranda's eyes. It tugged at Mateo's heart the way it had then, and at the same time guilt tightened inside him. It seemed like he had an awful lot to feel guilty about these days, and he had to wonder if maybe that said something about the way he'd been living his life. If maybe he should figure out what changes he needed to make to fix it.

No one seeing her work at the hospital, the picture of calm confidence, would guess at the insecurity that lay behind her professional mask. And that her mask had slipped because of the situation he'd placed her in here, reminding her of her difficult adolescence, made him feel angry and remorseful and determined to make it up to her.

"Miranda, I wish my parents had behaved differently. That you weren't feeling the way you are now. All I can say is that I think you're absolutely perfect, and anyone who doesn't see you for who you are, appreciate you for who you are, is a fool."

"Thank you. That's… That's a very sweet thing for you to say. And in case you don't know it, that's true for you, too."

Her words and expression loosened the band of guilt in his chest. Even in the darkness, he could see that the eyes looking up at him looked less forlorn. Shining with the amazing blue that startled him nearly every time he looked into them, and he found himself reaching for her before he'd even thought about it. Pulling her close, and as he did so, her lips parted. He wasn't sure what his intention had been, but seeing the look on her face gave him a very clear idea of exactly what he wanted to do now.

"It's not sweet. It's just true." And he lowered his head to kiss her.

"Your parents aren't out here now," she whispered, her breath feathering against his lips before his mouth connected with hers. "There's no need to kiss me."

"Believe me, I do need to kiss you. I've been thinking of little else since I kissed you before. From the moment I saw you standing here in the moonlight."

And because it was true, he did, wanting to taste again the soft lips he'd barely been able to pull back from when his parents had come into the room. For a long moment she stood there motionless, a little stiff, seeming to absorb what was happening between them, until he could feel her finally melt against him. A gasp left her mouth and swirled into his and she wrapped her arms around his neck and kissed him back. It was so good, so intoxicating, he found himself crushing her close, loving the feel of her lush, full breasts against his chest, the chemistry between them practically igniting the air as he deepened the kiss. Her body fit perfectly with his, and vague thoughts of secretly slipping to one of their rooms and making love with her short-circuited the back of his brain.

No. The thought both aroused and disturbed him. He'd asked her to come here as a friend, to help him. Not to push himself on her while she was feeling vulnerable, stuck at his parents' home with only him for company in the midst of their disapproving attitudes that had disturbed her so much.

He forced himself to pull back and look into the blue of her eyes which, even in the night air, he could tell were focused on him with the same turmoil and uncertainty he felt. Not sure exactly what to say, to explain what had just happened, he dropped his arms.

He couldn't do this. Miranda was doing a favor

for him by coming here with him. A bigger favor than he'd even realized, not knowing the lack of belonging and welcome she'd felt in the Davenport home, and now being subject to the same thing here.

Only a special woman who deeply cared about helping others would have agreed to this ruse, knowing his parents would probably be unhappy about their "engagement." What kind of rat would take advantage of her, kissing her and maybe even eventually making love with her, when, as far as he was concerned, their relationship would end as soon as they returned to the States in a week?

She'd admitted she'd like to have a family of her own someday, hadn't she? A husband who would be faithful and a home with children who loved their parents and one another. She hadn't had that growing up with a single mother, and while she now had a taste of that with her Davenport half-siblings, it was clear that having it all, belonging to a family that truly was all hers, was important to her.

And he was a man who could never give her that.

"I'm sorry. I hope you don't think I invited you here to be inappropriate with you. I'm not sure where that came from, but it won't happen again."

Confusion clouded her eyes, and he thrashed himself for being so weak as to kiss her when he shouldn't have. Had he hurt her feelings in the process? Reaching to hold her cold hand, he led the way back inside, not sure what exactly to do when they got there.

"Mateo."

"Yes?" He risked a glance down at her, relieved to see her expression was more normal now and, in fact, held some of the same determination he'd seen on the funicular earlier.

"I'd like to talk with your parents again. Have something to eat with them. It was silly of me to react the way I did. Part of the plan was to be engaged to a woman they wouldn't approve of, right? I'm fine with being that person. Really."

"Are you sure?" He studied her, wondering if keeping her here a few more days would be completely unfair. "I can't promise that my parents will magically be nice to you. In fact, I can guarantee that, right now, they're trying to figure out how to scare you off or change my mind. Stick me with some Catalonian girl who fits their criteria."

"Like I said, I can handle it. I survived moving into the Davenport mansion that was vibrating with disapproval when I was only sixteen, didn't I? If I could do that, I'm sure I can let your parents' dislike roll off my back."

"It didn't roll off twenty minutes ago."

"And I feel embarrassed about that. I'm a grown woman, not a child whose feelings get hurt at the least thing. I was being absurd, and I'm over it."

He looked at her closely, trying to decide the right and fair thing to do that wouldn't upset her any more. "It might still work for you to be angry with me and ditch me. I could play up having a broken heart to keep my parents' matchmaking at bay. Act wild and go out with a different woman every night, mortifying my parents so much they'd be happy to see the back of me returning to the States for a while."

"Would that work?" Her lips quirked. "I have to wonder if that's always been your MO, and everyone's used to it already."

He'd only been partly joking about seeing other women, since that strategy might actually work. But looking at the curve of her lips, the cute way she shook her head at him, he knew Miranda was the woman he wanted to spend time with here. There was something about the way she'd faced her fear on the ride up the mountainside, the way her intelligent mind worked, the way she smiled and laughed, that made the thought of spending time with anyone else seem utterly unappealing.

"Not exactly my MO. My wildness only comes

out on occasions that warrant it." And there it came again. That shimmer of awareness, the chemistry that had zinged between them from practically the moment they'd met, was crackling all around them, and he knew he had to cool it before he did something he'd regret.

Like drag her to his room and make love with her all night, forgetting all about the reason they'd come here in the first place.

Mateo breathed deeply and picked up the pace to the house, forcing his mind away from thoughts of hot sex that kept interrupting his good intentions to keep it strictly friendly between them. "So, what's it to be?" he asked, somehow managing to make his voice sound calmly conversational. "I can have the Alves jet ready to fly later tonight or tomorrow morning. Or we can go back and talk to my parents more, setting the tone for this trip and my life. Giving them hints that they shouldn't expect me to move back permanently, at the same time reassuring them that I'm planning to take on at least some of the responsibility they're worried about."

"I'm in," Miranda said firmly. "I just realized with certainty that I'm not done adventuring here and trying to be at least a little crazy. I can do this. My sister Penny would be proud that I'm not bailing out."

"*Gracias.* I'm proud of you, too." He brought

her cold hand to his lips and, after a long moment, forced himself to let go. "Tonight, we'll deal with my parents together. Steel ourselves for the party they'd already planned with a number of friends tomorrow night, which now will be a vehicle to announce our engagement. To try to take our minds off how awful that's going to be, we'll spend tomorrow adventuring again, okay? I think you'll enjoy what I have planned."

"You said that about Montserrat, completely leaving out details of the funicular flying through outer space up the mountain."

"Do you trust me, Miranda?"

Her eyes met his for a long time before she smiled, then said softly, "Yes, Mateo Alves. Yes, I think I do. I do."

"Bueno." His chest felt lighter at her answer, and he couldn't help but drop a soft kiss to her lips one more time. "I promise not to let you down."

Miranda wasn't sure what all the emotions were that swirled around in her chest and belly. Excitement? Yes. Who wouldn't be, getting to spend another glorious afternoon with Mateo in amazing Spain?

But discomfort squiggled its way in there, too. Last night had been so strange, meeting his parents, Mateo upset with them, kissing her breathless, then backing off, clearly regretting that he had, even as he'd asked her to spend today with him.

Which made her regret the kiss, too. The last thing she wanted was to be worryingly attracted to a man who wanted to be "just friends." Except the way her heart fluttered as she combed her hair into the neat bob she kept it in told her that maybe it was too late. But she was no slave to her hormones, right? She could be friends with Mateo, and not want anything else. Couldn't she? A fierce little inner voice told her there was no question about it. The man was way out of her league, and falling for him would just set her up for heartache.

Mateo had refused to tell her what he'd planned for them to do this morning, just advising her to dress warmly and to bring extra layers, which was intriguing. Obviously, they were going to do something outdoors. Hopefully it wasn't anything more daring than hiking this time. She'd loved seeing Montserrat, but thinking about that funicular ride still gave her palpitations, as did anticipating what he had in mind, and whether or not it might include more kissing. Which, of course, it wouldn't, and why was she even thinking about it?

He'd been sure to keep his distance from her the rest of last night, even in front of his parents.

No more kissing or touching, just that *I'm so in love with you* look he kept giving her that was impressively convincing. Maybe that look was what kept stirring her all up, even when she'd scolded herself to stop. She knew what this game was about, and deluding herself it could be anything else was just stupid.

Dinner with the Alveses had been awkward at best, but at least they'd been civil toward her. Less civil toward Mateo, which was hard to understand, and made Miranda glad she'd come to support him, no matter how odd and uncomfortable it felt to play this charade. How could they seem to disapprove of him so much? He'd served in the military, helping save lives. Then had honed those and other skills in the U.S., helping more people. And he'd come back as they'd asked, trying to find a balance between how he wanted to live his life and his obligations to family and their role here.

Yet, by the way they spoke to him, you'd think he was living his life as a frivolous playboy, off spending his family's wealth.

The part of her that saw such innate strength in the man told her that seemed impossible. But he'd fully admitted he didn't want to come home, and they'd always been able to rely on Emilio. Was part of the reason for that because he himself believed he didn't measure up to his brother?

She shook her head. It was true she didn't really know him, except that she knew he was good at his job. And it wouldn't be surprising if "playboy" fit into his lifestyle somewhere, since she was positive most women would fall into his arms at the least invitation. Hadn't she been one of them?

To her shock, she had, and the memories of that brought hot color to her face. Thinking bad thoughts at his apartment, then falling into his kisses so deeply she'd nearly forgotten how to breathe. Which was beyond embarrassing, since the first time he'd kissed her, he'd done it for his parents' benefit. And the second time? Who knew what that had been about, but the way he'd instantly backed off had told her loud and clear that it hadn't been because he felt the same pull she did. Maybe it was that playboy thing, and he always kissed any woman he was close to in a dark garden lit by a fingernail moon. And hadn't she learned that playboy types, or men wanting to date her for her Davenport connections, weren't to be trusted? Not with her heart, at least.

This whole thing is a charade, remember, Miranda? she scolded herself. *Not. Real.*

She huffed out a sigh and stepped down the beautifully decorated stairs to find Mateo waiting for her by the front door, as he'd promised, giving her a warm smile. Paula was standing patiently next to him, holding a pair of leather boots and beaming. Her expression helped Miranda relax and smile, too. At least one person in this house seemed to like her, and was happy for Mateo. Too bad her happiness would be dashed in the very near future when they broke off their "engagement."

"We're lucky to have a beautiful day," Mateo said. "Ready to get some fresh air and see more of the beauty of northern Spain?"

"I'm ready. Though I know there's skiing in the Pyrenees, and I'm hoping that you telling me to wear warm layers isn't because you're planning on us doing that, because I don't know how."

"Not today. Though I'm happy to teach you to ski tomorrow, if you like."

"No, thanks. I'm beginning to see that my desire to be adventurous is battling with the wimpy side of me I didn't realize was there." Embarrassingly true. Which was one more reason she was glad she'd agreed to come, despite everything. Definitely past time to push herself out of her cocoon a little more. "Tell me what you have planned, so I can stop worrying. Or start worrying, depending on what it is."

Paula looked up at a chuckling Mateo. "You are taking Dr. Davenport paragliding, yes? Show her the beautiful scenery of the area of my birth?

I know that has always been a favorite pastime of yours. She will love it."

"No, Paula. My fiancée is not fond of heights." Mateo's smile flat-lined and he took the boots from the housekeeper's hands. "We'll just be hiking. Thank you for bringing her some boots."

"I am sorry, Mr. Mateo. I… I should have realized," Paula said, now looking upset and worried, her smile gone. "I know that it hasn't been very long, and—"

"It's fine, Paula. Are you ready, Miranda?"

He helped her with her coat before leading her to his car, and as they drove in silence she had to wonder about his exchange with Paula. The way he'd interrupted, then dismissed the woman's words seemed very unlike him. Coupled with the expression on his face, which could only be described as grim, and Paula's obvious distress, it was clear something was bothering him.

"We'll be driving through parts of the Parque Nacional de Ordesa y Monte Perdido—our national park. Then hiking some of the beautiful trails. Don't worry." His teeth flashed in a smile, banishing some of the grimness as they drove down the winding road from his parents' estate. "We'll stay in the lower elevations and off the cliffs. It's too late in the season to go on the high roads, which are likely covered in snow.

But you'll enjoy the panoramic views and communing with nature, I promise."

"Sounds wonderful. This trip is helping me see that I spend way too much time in the city, and shut inside the busy hospital. Breathing fresh air and having nature all around me sounds like the perfect getaway." Especially with Mateo Alves to look at along with the mountains and valleys. She'd admire him the same way, with a detached appreciation for beauty. She could do that. If she tried hard enough.

"*Bueno*. Paula has packed us a picnic lunch. Hopefully it's warm enough to enjoy it outdoors, but if it's too cold, we'll make it a car picnic, if that's all right with you?"

"So long as we're not hanging up in the sky from a funicular, hang-glider, or ski lift, anything and everything is all right with me."

"I'll put that in my reference notes. Everything is fine with you except hanging from the sky— does that almost sound like a song lyric to you? I think I'll compose that, and title it 'Miranda in the Sky with Diamonds'." He grinned and reached across the console to tap the ring he'd given her to wear as part of their ruse.

"I think that song's sort of taken. And the diamond isn't really mine."

"All right, how about 'Miranda's eyes are like

diamonds the color of the sky.' How's that for romantic?"

"Save it for when your parents are around to hear it. And who knew you had mad skills like song-writing to add to your résumé?" She kept her voice light, fighting down the silly flutter in her tummy when he talked about romance. And why was he? He'd made it clear last night he didn't think of her in that way. Or, at least, didn't want to. Flirting probably just came as naturally to the man as breathing, which she would do well to remember, and not read any meaning into it.

He gave her that grin that made her stomach flutter annoyingly even more, then sent the car through mountain passes at speeds that would have thrilled Penny, but had Miranda clutching her seat and holding her breath. She knew if she asked, he'd slow down, but hadn't she decided that it was past time to live her life a little more on the edge? This trip was certainly accomplishing that in more ways than one.

Mateo told her about the old and charming towns, as well as educating her on the geographic elements they passed. She gazed in wonder, thinking how incredible it would be to live here. She knew Mateo's reasons for moving to New York, but had to admit that the longer she was here, the harder it was for her to imagine he'd planned to leave all this behind forever, until the tragedy of his brother's death was forcing him to modify that plan.

"The hiking trail along the river is the easiest, but still beautiful," Mateo said as the road ended in a parking area. "I figured you weren't up for a long trek up the steepest trails, though the views are incredible from there."

"I appreciate that. I'd probably be sucking wind on a steep trail."

"You definitely need to get out of the hospital more. I see you practically every time I'm there."

"Maybe." It was true, she probably did work too much, but taking extra shifts was one more way to try to prove she was worthy of the Davenport name. Not to mention that dating wasn't high on her list of things to do. She'd learned the hard way that they either didn't like the work hours she kept, or they figured that she was the key to a fortune, and didn't really care for her personally at all. Not trusting a man's attention or words of love to be real was something she'd eventually taken to heart.

Mateo got their gear out of the trunk of the car and set everything on metal benches next to the parking area. Shoving her feet into the hiking boots was a bit of a challenge, but after she got them laced, she stole a look at the man sitting next to her. At his strong jaw, thick black hair, and sensual lips that brought back memories of their searing kisses.

Aside from his obvious sex appeal, she had to wonder if his status as the heir to a dukedom was one of the reasons she found herself so drawn to him? He had family money of his own, and wouldn't be interested in hers. Plus he'd said loud and clear that he wasn't looking for a long-term commitment with any woman. Which made him safe to spend a little time with, right? She didn't have to worry about impressing him in hope of something more.

The thought made her frown. Safe. Impressing others. Was her whole life focused on those two things? Keeping herself safe from heartache and pain? Safe from criticism by accomplishing things people expected of a Davenport? Safe from the hazards of the world, to the point where she wrapped herself in cotton wool to insulate herself?

"You're scowling." He leaned closer, his fingertip smoothing across her forehead. "Are you not wanting to hike? We can just have our picnic here, if you like, then drive some more and see the various views from the road."

"No." Miranda looked into Mateo's eyes, then noticed him shoving the backpack that presumably held their lunch to the end of the bench. Her heart warmed at his consideration—when was the last time she'd spent time with such a sweet and thoughtful man, who seemed to really want to do whatever made her happy and comfortable? "I'm just thinking about the way I've been living my life. Maybe this trip was meant to help me take a look at that in a way I haven't been doing."

"And how have you been living your life, other than working too much?"

"I guess I've been worried too much about trying to impress people. Prove I might be worthy of the Davenport name. Not put myself in situations that might be scary or potentially hurtful. I… Maybe I've been living my life as a coward."

"A coward? Now, there's a word no one would ever use about you, Miranda. Aren't you the woman who braved going into a collapsing tunnel? Who went up the funicular, even though it scared you? Who came on this trip with me after barely knowing me and having no idea how it would go?"

"I guess." His words, along with the admiring smile in his eyes, had her smiling back, even though she tried not to put too much trust into all he was saying. But a warm little glow filled her chest anyway. "Maybe it's being around you that makes me feel more brave than usual, putting myself in situations I normally wouldn't. So thank you for that."

He smiled and gently flicked his warm finger beneath her chin. "So I don't need to feel so guilty about dragging you here to terrify you on the funicular and have to deal with my parents?"

"Like I told you last night, I'm here by choice, and you know what? I'm ready to hit the trail."

"Bueno." He shrugged on the backpack, enfolded her hand in his, and they set off.

The farther they walked, the more Miranda was amazed at the beauty surrounding them. Tall beech trees, maples with a few gold and red leaves left, the beauty of the rocky cliffs and the valley, with trout clearly visible in the glassy river as they trekked beside it.

"This is incredible! I didn't know what to expect, but this is beyond anything I'd imagined. Living in big cities for my whole life, I guess I've forgotten how wonderful it is to enjoy nature and open spaces like this. I feel… I feel at peace here, you know?"

"Do you?" He paused, seeming struck by the comment. "I guess I always did too. Whenever I felt buried by schoolwork, or my family was driving me crazy, I'd come out here."

"How did your family drive you crazy back then? Did you and Emilio have sibling squabbles?"

"Of course." A smile twisted his lips. "But Emilio and I were close, and did a lot of things together. I only got a little jealous when my parents favored him so much, but it wasn't his fault. And honestly? He deserved most of the admiration they gave him."

"How did they favor him?"

"In lots of ways. Hey, look!" He pointed to the sky. "See the eagles? If you pay attention you might see vultures, too, all looking for their lunch."

It seemed clear he didn't want to keep talking about his brother and the Alves family dynamics. "Wow, that's incredible. I've never seen an eagle before. The way they fly and glide is magnificent, isn't it?"

"There are ways humans can fly here, too, Miranda. Base jumping, hang-gliding, parasailing."

"Um, thanks, but you already know I'll leave the hanging in the sky to the birds. Parasailing and all that looks too dangerous, as far as wimpy me is concerned."

To her surprise, he suddenly looked somber, instead of amused, at their banter. What had she said to make him look like that?

"This looks like a good place for our lunch break," Mateo said as they walked on in sudden silence. He stopped to gesture at a large, flat rock jutting from the hillside by the path. "Are you hungry?"

"Famished. I can't remember being this hungry before."

The dark eyes staring into hers held an odd expression. Miranda wasn't sure what it was, she only knew that her breathless feeling came back in spades and her heart beat a little faster.

"I can't either, *mi belleza.*"

His gaze lingered on hers, and just as she felt she was drowning in it, he turned away to drop the backpack onto the rock. Miranda couldn't believe the containers of foods and sandwiches he pulled out, making her mouth water—or was it Mateo that had done that? Thoughts of kissing his beautiful mouth, tasting him again, suddenly seemed even more appealing than lunch, fool that she was.

With the food laid out, his gaze met hers again before dropping to her mouth. Mesmerized, she felt her lips part in anticipation. His face slowly lowered and his mouth met hers, soft and sweet and delicious.

The sound of voices coming from down the trail jerked Miranda back to reality as their lips parted, and she quickly looked down, pretending to decide on a sandwich. Wow, she needed to get her thoughts back on track. If he wanted a quick affair with her, he'd already be pursuing that, wouldn't he? Instead, he'd backed off each time they'd kissed, or come close to kissing.

Surely she had enough pride not to want a man who didn't particularly want her, didn't she? And she was well aware that a simple kiss on a rock in the middle of nature didn't mean a thing. So why did she keep trying to make it mean something it didn't?

The family passed by, two parents with three children, the youngest looking only three or so years old. They smiled and spoke in Spanish to Mateo, and he answered back.

"I really need to study Spanish," Miranda said as she picked up a sandwich. "It would be helpful when treating Hispanic patients in the hospital."

"It is very helpful. Some of the EMTs even call me to translate if I'm not on a run with them."

"So, was that family envious of all this food?" she asked, trying to bring back the pleasant normalcy they'd been enjoying before, squashing the heat she'd felt vibrating between them. Vibrating from her end at least. But she just couldn't seem to help it.

"They said they'd just enjoyed theirs, so I thankfully didn't feel a need to offer them some."

"Looks like Paula packed enough for them and us, too."

He smiled. "She always fussed over Emilio and me when we were kids. Almost like a second mother to us, you know?"

"How long has she been with your family?"

"As long as I can remember. Raised her own brood, and us, too. All of her adult children now work somewhere on the estate."

"That's really wonderful, having a connection like that."

"I guess it is." He looked at her as though he hadn't thought about that before. "I took it for granted, growing up with it. It's like having a huge, extended family, I suppose. I need to meet with some of them before we go back to New York, talk about the most pressing things that need to be dealt with now that Emilio's gone."

"Are you going to try to address some of it while you're here?"

"I don't know. First, I have to find out if things are in good shape or not so good. So, how's the food?"

Again, a change of subject. Miranda wondered if he didn't want to think about the weight of his family's expectations in running the estate, or the loss of his brother, or both. She was coming to realize even more how many really tough things he had to deal with right now, and she was glad all over again that she'd come, if her being here helped even a little.

"Speaking of family, I haven't told you. I got a message that Charles is engaged."

"Your brother? Is this good news, or bad?"

Trust a man who never wanted to marry to ask

that question. "It's wonderful news. He's been very alone since his wife died, spending all his spare time taking care of his twin boys. And he's marrying Grace Forbes, another ER doc you probably know. I'm really happy for both of them."

"Well, if you're happy, I guess that's good."

His expression showed he couldn't really imagine an engagement—a real one—being good.

They ate in silence for a while, listening to the sound of the river gently swirling by and the birds chattering in the trees. Even though he'd changed the subject several times, would it help Mateo if he talked a little more about his brother? Maybe offering him her ear was what a friend should do.

"Your brother," she said quietly. "How did he die?"

"Doing something we both loved to do. That we spent a lot of time doing together."

"How does that make you feel?"

"The way he died was the result of being very reckless. And I have to wonder if I'd been more in touch with him, talked with him about the problems in his life, that might have helped him feel more at peace. I don't know, but I do know that being here makes it feel more real than when I was in New York. It seems impossible that he's not here any more, where everywhere I turn, there are memories of him."

"Oh, Mateo." She wrapped her arms around him and gathered him close. "I'm so sorry that you lost him."

He pulled her close and pressed his cheek to hers. The long, silent connection made her realize it was the first time he'd really talked about it to her. Had accepted comfort from her. And that made anything his parents had to say to her much less important.

Slowly, he eased away. "So am I. For a lot of reasons. But being sorry won't bring him back." He gathered up the remnants of their lunch and stuck them in the backpack. "Ready to move on? There's a waterfall not too much farther on that I know you'll like to see."

Clearly, the subject was again closed. But at least he'd opened up a little, and that was a start.

"A waterfall sounds wonderful." The bleakness, the pain she could see in the depths of his eyes had her reaching to cup his cheek in her palm. "Just remember that I know well how much it hurts to lose someone you loved dearly. That it's the kind of pain that takes years to heal. The pain of losing my mother is still with me, and I have a feeling I'll miss her, miss getting to share important things in my life with her, forever."

He nodded, turning his head to press his mouth against her palm. "Talking with you is making me realize I can't keep just shoving it down and pretending it isn't there, when being home just brings it to the surface anyway. It's time to start dealing with it, I guess. I'm just not sure how."

He tugged her close against him and she lifted her mouth to his, intending the kiss to be comforting, to show she cared and was here for him, a chaste kiss before she pulled back. But his palms came up to her face and he kissed her slowly, sweetly, until one hand slipped into her hair and tilted her head back, deepening the kiss. Making her feel weak in the knees and way too hot in all her clothing layers, and she clutched the heavy coat covering his wide shoulders to keep from melting to the ground.

A piercing shriek, then alarmed shouts came from quite a distance away, sending their lips popping apart and both their heads swiveling toward the sound. There was no sign of anyone on the path, but as the shrieking grew even louder, Mateo took off running. Miranda, her heart pounding and already out of breath from that kiss and from trying to catch up with him, focused on getting to whoever needed help without breaking her neck on the stones and tree roots trying to trip up her feet as she ran.

CHAPTER EIGHT

THE SHRIEKS WERE eerily similar to the way Emily had sounded after falling from her father's shoulders, and Mateo knew it must be one of the children that had passed by earlier, or possibly a different family coming from the opposite direction. He knew not to panic, but also knew it could be something serious, and the only way to find out what they might be dealing with was to get there fast.

Miranda followed him, but he couldn't hear the sound of her steps anymore. Whatever had happened, he and Miranda could deal with a medical emergency. And if it was more than that, if there was some kind of rescue needed, he always came prepared.

Rounding a curve in the path, he saw the woman they'd seen before clutching two of the children close to her sides as she stared down the steep embankment toward the river, crying out to whoever was below. Mateo ran up next to her, looking down to see that the man who had passed them earlier was picking his way down, sliding at times as he went.

"Hang on!" the man yelled, obviously panicked. "I'm coming to get you. Don't let go!"

Mateo's chest tightened when he saw the gravity of the situation. The tiniest child was hanging on with only one arm to a scrubby, leafless bush growing straight from the side of the embankment, his feet and other arm dangling and swaying over the river. The water wasn't running fast enough to take the child downstream very quickly, but if he fell? He definitely could suffer a serious injury on the rocks below.

"I've got a rope." Mateo pulled the deceptively thin line from his pocket and moved toward the embankment, working as fast as he could to wrap and secure one end around a sturdy tree.

"Oh, my God, will that hold both of you?" The woman stared up him with wide, terrified eyes.

"Don't worry, it's stronger than it looks." One last wrap, and it was ready. "I'll get the child. Stay where you are," he yelled to the man below, "because you're as likely to fall as he is." He knew too well how true that was. He couldn't count how many times a second person, or more, had lost their footing trying to help someone else.

"Oh, my God, please help them," the mother

cried as he unrolled the line and began to rappel down to the boy.

"I'm almost there. I can get him and hand him up to you," the man said, grabbing a root to stop from sliding before staring up at Mateo with wild eyes.

It was never good to have the rescuer as freaked out as the one in danger. "Let me. I'm a search and rescue specialist, and an EMT. You can trust me to get him, I promise. Stay right there."

Doubtless because Mateo had already moved past the man, he stayed there, gripping the root. When he got parallel to the boy, Mateo braced his leg against the rocky embankment, grasped the rope tightly with one hand, then curled his free arm around the child, holding him close to his body.

"I've got you, okay? Don't be scared, and don't look down. Are those your parents up there?"

The boy kept crying, but nodded through his tears, clutching at Mateo's coat.

"Look at them, okay? Wrap your arms around my neck and hold tight. All set? Up we go now."

Mateo wanted to make sure the child didn't look down at the river and get so scared he tried to loosen himself from Mateo's grip. That seemed counterintuitive, but he'd had more than one soldier or patient do exactly that, making it very hard to hold onto them, but at least this little guy probably weighed only thirty or so pounds.

"You stay there," Mateo commanded the father as he pulled himself and the boy up the rope, passing him. He'd learned that sounding firm and authoritative was important in this kind of situation, when people were panicking and not thinking straight. "I'll send it down for you after he's safe. Don't move."

The man nodded, stilling hanging onto the root, and Mateo prayed it would keep holding him for a few more minutes. He looked up to see if the mother was ready to take the boy, or if he'd need to bring him all the way over the ledge. Miranda was standing there, her arms open, reaching instead as the mother kept her other two safely away from the edge.

"Ready for me to hand him over?" Mateo asked as, with one more hard pull, his head rose above the ledge. "Don't try to take him straight from my arms. Let me get his bottom safely sitting before you take over."

"Got it."

Mateo reached to sit the kid on the ledge, and the moment he seemed secure there, Miranda had her arms around the child. She dragged him away from the edge until he was a good four feet from it, and Mateo was surprised to hear him start to cry even harder when the mother rushed over to him and Miranda and pulled him into her arms.

Mateo hauled himself up and over the ledge to stand by the tree. Barely glancing at the howling child, he turned to look down at the father, knowing Miranda was more than capable of handling whatever the problem was with the boy.

"Ready to catch the rope? When you do, pull yourself up with a hand-over-hand movement. On the count of three—one, two three." Relieved that his first attempt at tossing the rope went straight to his hands, he and the man worked together. The guy slowly heaved himself up, jamming his feet into the rocks for leverage, and at the same time Mateo helped by pulling on the rope as he climbed. In a matter of minutes he was scrambling over the ledge and Mateo grabbed him by the armpits to help him get to safety. Obviously shaken, he stood and pumped Mateo's hand.

"Thank you. Thank you so much," he gasped.

"You okay?"

The man nodded, catching his breath, then frowned when he saw their little boy was still extremely upset. "Is he hurt?" he asked, looking first at Mateo then at his wife. "Or is he just still scared?"

Mateo turned to see Miranda, who'd moved far away from the ledge and was carefully checking the boy. She was now every inch the calm, medical professional who would make any worried parent feel better, and not the sexy, vibrant woman he'd been unable to resist kissing not long ago. Then he realized she had no idea what the parents were saying and needed to connect them all.

"This is Dr. Davenport, she's an emergency room doctor in the States. She doesn't speak Spanish, but I'll interpret as soon as she finishes her exam. Miranda," he said, switching to English, "can you tell what's going on? Find anything?"

"One more minute." Miranda carefully wrapped her fingers around the child's arm, and received a scream in response. She glanced up at him, then smiled at the parents. "See the way he's holding his arm close to his tummy? Tell them I'm almost positive this is nursemaid's elbow, which isn't serious. Can you ask if one of them yanked on his arm as he was falling off the path?"

Mateo did as she asked, and, sure enough, they confirmed that the dad had grabbed the boy's arm, trying to pull him up, but he'd slipped from his grasp.

"All right," Miranda said. "Please ask one of the parents to hold him in their lap. I'm going to check it again, then, assuming that's it, I'll pop the radius back into place. You have anything to distract him while I do that?"

If the boy had been a grown man, he'd say that Miranda and her calm, friendly demeanor, gorgeous blue eyes and disheveled hair, which he realized he liked as much as her carefully combed bob, were plenty of distraction on their own. "I have a whistle in my pocket. Let's see if he wants to blow it."

Her smile widened, and he loved the twinkle in her eyes. "That's perfect. Wish I could use a whistle at the hospital, but probably other patients wouldn't appreciate it. Is mom or dad ready?"

Mateo spoke with the parents, and the dad took over the two older ones as the mother held the child close in her arms. Now that he was looking, he could see the boy's arm was hanging limply at his side.

"Now I see why he was holding onto that bush with only one arm. Which was nerve-racking, let me tell you. I thought he might lose his grip and fall before I got there. But don't tell his parents."

"They already know you're a hero, so why keep that a secret?"

"Because heroes are never scared, don't you know that?"

She shook her head and grinned at him before turning to carefully palpate the boy's entire arm, with shrieks that made his parents cringe following each movement.

"Yep, that's definitely it," Miranda said. "Whistle time. Tell the parents to expect a loud scream, then he'll be feeling fine, just a little bruised."

Mateo translated again, and the boy was, thankfully, fascinated by the whistle. As he was blasting everyone's ears, Mateo watched Miranda gently tug on his arm, and even through the whistling he could hear the bone pop back into place. As expected, the boy screamed, the parents exclaimed in distress, then visibly relaxed when the boy's misery quieted to mere sniffles.

"You're good with that whistle, young man," Mateo said, trying to distract all of them now that the worst was over. "You want to keep it?"

He nodded, and when he began to blow it again, his parents laughed, obviously relieved. They thanked both he and Miranda over and over again, the mother giving her a hard hug as Mateo re-rolled his rigging and placed it back in his pocket.

"I bet they're going to hang on to all three of them all the way back to wherever they're parked," Miranda said with a smile as she watched them move down the path. "How scary to see their little one fall over the embankment like that. I wonder what happened?"

"Kids can move fast. One second they're walking on a sidewalk, or in this case a path in the woods, the next they've darted into the street or off the edge. I see it all the time."

"I know. I regularly see the results of kids' impulsiveness in the ER. I guess there's no way to keep everyone safe all the time, is there?"

"No." His chest got that heavy feeling again, as her words sent him back to their earlier conversation. Some accidents—fatal accidents—were incomprehensible. Seemingly impossible. But when they happened, everyone else had to live through the tragedy, wondering what they might have done to prevent it.

"I guess we'd better go back and gather up the picnic stuff before it attracts bears and we have another problem on our hands," Miranda said. "And as I say that, I hope you're going to tell me there aren't really any bears here."

The way her eyes had gone from grinning to questioning and slightly worried brought him out of the dark place he'd gone. "*Ursus arctos*—brown bears—definitely live here. And I'm thankful for that, as there are very few left, and they're an important part of our great wilderness."

"I'm all for brown bears being part of your wilderness, but not if they show up when I'm hiking."

"I can't disagree with that. Let's gather up our stuff and go. I think I've had enough excitement for one day. You?"

"Definitely yes. And by the way, you were amazing. When I saw how fast you rappelled down that embankment, and how calmly you got the boy and brought him back up, I couldn't believe it. You really are an expert at rescuing people, aren't you? They were so lucky to have you close by."

"To have ER doc extraordinaire Miranda Davenport here, too. Diagnosing his injury and fixing it also made them very lucky."

"Anyone at any hospital could have fixed his arm, including you. Not too many could have rescued him the way you did."

The blue eyes looking up at him were utterly serious now, and something about the way she was looking at him gave him an odd sensation. A little uncomfortable at accolades he didn't need to hear—he did what he did because it was his calling. A little bit proud, too, despite not needing that kind of praise. And a little confused at the first thing that came to mind when she'd said all that was that they worked remarkably well together. Both when it came to taking care of patients and when it came to enjoying time together in a way he couldn't quite remember enjoying so much with anyone before.

"We make a good team." He hadn't meant to say it out loud, but there it was, hanging between them. Words that felt bigger and more significant than a simple statement about working together.

"Yeah, we do."

Mateo stared down to see the same confusion in her eyes that swirled through his mind and body. Let his gaze travel to her lush lips, down to the pulse he could see beating in her throat just above her coat collar, and couldn't believe he felt so aroused when he wasn't even touching her and both of them wore heavy clothes covering nearly every inch of their skin.

After each kiss they'd shared, he'd promised himself it would be the last. And yet, at this moment, he wanted to do nothing more than lie down on the hard rock slab they'd picnicked on and kiss her breathless.

Damn. How had this gotten so complicated and confusing? He'd dreaded coming back home, but being with Miranda had made it so much better than he'd imagined it would be. Seeing his home through her eyes, as well as parts of Catalonia he hadn't visited for years, made him feel completely different than he'd expected. Filled him with pleasure and happy memories, and not just the painful ones he'd known he'd have to deal with. It had brought a smile and joy to his heart to spend time with a woman who enjoyed simple pleasures like hiking and picnicking. Kissing and holding each other close.

Much as he knew he shouldn't be doing that kissing and holding, there was something irresistible about Miranda. Maybe it was the combination of sweetness and smarts, of vulnerability and bravery, of caring and giving that was a soul-deep part of her.

Whatever it was, he knew he didn't want the day with her to end with their hike. The enjoyment to be over before they had to deal with going to the party, where he'd have to answer questions he didn't want to answer. Where there'd be hushed conversations about Emilio being gone, and about Mateo not being the kind of man his brother had been. About what would happen now.

He didn't want to think about all that quite yet, and looked down into Miranda's beautiful face. "It's early still. How do you feel about a little tour of part of the estate as I talk to a few managers before we have to get ready for the party? There's probably more to do than I realize, and I should get started scheduling meetings with them now, and not wait."

"I'd love that. It's all so beautiful to see from the guest house. Looking at it up close, learning about all you raise and grow there, about the horses and all the different livestock, would be really interesting."

"*Bueno.* We'll take an hour or so to do a quick tour while I set up times to meet with everyone before we have to get ready for tonight."

"Well, this makes me happy." He could tell from her shining eyes and wide smile that she really meant it, and somehow her excitement had him looking forward to it, too. "I admit I wanted to see more of the place, but didn't know if I'd just be in the way."

"You could never be in the way. Having you with me will make a difficult task easier." *In the way?* That she'd actually say that bothered him. How could such a special woman still carry around those kinds of worries that must stem from her early years at the Davenports?

He reached for her hand and drew her closer. "You'll have to keep your boots on, as trudging through fields will be part of it. And climbing olive trees. And walking across barn beams."

Her chuckle and laughing eyes reached inside him, making him feel grateful all over again that she was here. Knew that having her with him for at least a little of this necessary task would help him get through it. He was sure the various estate managers could handle taking over all the things Emilio wasn't here to do anymore. In fact, they'd probably all prefer to do it themselves, instead of working with him if he tried to fill his brother's shoes.

No way could he come close to doing all the things his brother had accomplished here. And he was sure they all knew he couldn't either, despite what his parents claimed to believe.

"Look at all the olives on these trees! How many acres…er…hectares of olive groves do you have?" Miranda asked as they walked between the rows of trees, now more gnarled-looking than Mateo remembered, on their way to the horse barns.

"Not sure exactly what we have anymore." He'd talked earlier to several of the livestock managers, but hadn't yet spoken to those who took care of the various crops. "But in the past, not a huge number. The olives we grow here have mostly been eaten by everyone living on the estate, with about two thirds of the crop pressed into oil."

"How do you press it?"

"There's a local press that all the nearby orchards use. The harvest is taken to be processed pretty much the same way it's been done for hundreds of years."

"When is it harvested? And how? There's no way you could pick all these tiny olives off the trees—it would take forever."

He chuckled at the way she stared at the trees,

reaching to touch the silvery gray leaves and not yet ripe olives before running her hand over the rough bark. "You're such a city girl, with an inquisitive mind. The harvest will be soon. Probably in the next month or two, depending on the weather. They're raked off the tree onto nets."

"What? You rake them off?"

"Yes, and I know from personal experience how hard it is. By the end of the day your shoulders and back muscles are groaning big time." He smiled at the memories of Emilio and himself complaining like mad, even though they both secretly liked the labor of pulling the olives from the trees. "Our parents insisted that Emilio and I do some of the raking, even though most of our friends on neighboring estates never had to. They felt we needed that personal connection with the land, and our home. Be a real part of it all."

Miranda turned to look at him, and he could practically read her mind, because his words struck him exactly the same way.

A personal connection. A real part of it all. Walking across the land of his ancestors, he couldn't deny that, for the past couple days, he'd been filled with powerful memories of his childhood. Happy memories of how much this place had always meant to him, until he'd realized he had to forge his own path away from here. Even the memories of Emilio and himself doing things together brought a smile to his lips, along with the ache of loss.

"And your personal connection to the horses? You told me you and your brother spent a lot of time here."

They'd arrived at the paddock, with a few of their horses inside. One whinnied at them, and as he reached to rub the animal's nose, Mateo's chest filled with some kind of emotion he couldn't quite identify. It had been a long time since he'd ridden a horse, and he suddenly knew he wanted to make that happen before he went back to New York.

"We did. Again, my parents made us do some of the mucking out and feeding. Said we couldn't have just the fun of riding, we had to do some of the work, too."

Miranda moved close to him, pressing her shoulder to his arm. "You love this place, don't you? Admit it."

He could feel her looking at him, and finally turned to meet her serious gaze. How she could see that so clearly, when he hadn't, had refused to, was a mystery.

But she was right.

"I guess I do. I grew up here. It's in my blood, I suppose. But loving the land and the animals and the beauty doesn't mean I belong here any more. My job in New York helps me make a difference in other people's lives."

"Have you thought about how this place makes a difference in people's lives?"

"What do you mean?"

"All the people who work here. Who live here. You said they were like family, didn't you? Without this place, their lives would change completely. They'd all have to find work on other horse farms, other olive farms, other places that raise the livestock you do."

He stared out across the fields. Miranda was right, and yet it didn't really change anything. "Emilio worked to make sure this whole place ran like a well-oiled machine. Nothing will change with him gone."

Except everything had changed. This place would never be the same without him, and the thought of living here in his brother's big shadow, facing grief and guilt every day, felt unbearable.

"Mateo." She grasped his hands, and just that touch made him feel a little steadier. "Perhaps you need to take a little more time to think about everything. That's what our pretend engagement's really all about anyway, right? To give your parents time to adjust to their new situation without demanding you do exactly what they want. To give yourself time to figure out how you want to handle it."

"I don't need more time to know that I can't take Emilio's place. And, deep inside, I have to believe my parents know that, too."

"Being yourself will always be enough. Remember that."

Her words squeezed his heart, and he folded her in his arms. "You seem to have trouble believing that about yourself, Miranda."

"Yeah, maybe I do," she whispered as she wrapped her arms around his back and held him close. "Maybe that's something we can both work on, hmm?"

"Yeah." He pressed his lips to her warm cheek, calling upon all his strength not to move on to her sweet lips. "And tonight's party will be a good place for us to start."

CHAPTER NINE

"I HOPE THE dresses fit, Miss Miranda," Paula said, showing her to a guest room in the main house for her to change in. "Mr. Mateo wanted you to have several to choose from. He asked me to tell you to wear whichever you like best."

"I admit the dress I brought isn't quite this fancy, but it's adequate, I think."

"Mr. Mateo wanted you to feel comfortable at the party, not worrying about your clothes. He made a special effort to get them for you. Miss Camilla never liked the dresses her husband chose for her, and I know it made him sad."

She looked at the woman in surprise, wondering why she'd mentioned Emilio's widow. "It bothered him?"

A shadow crossed Paula's face. "Yes. But he tried very hard to make Miss Camilla happy."

Miranda felt a flash of anger at the self-centered woman who'd hurt Mateo's brother, and who was part of the reason Mateo had kept such a distance between himself and his family for so long. From the place he'd admitted today that he loved very much. "Were Emilio and Mateo close?"

"Oh, yes. Very close. When they were both home, they did everything together. Rode the horses, skied, sailed boats, and—"

She abruptly stopped talking, and Miranda prodded, "And?"

"And many other things." Paula moved to the dresses and smoothed the skirts. "So, please, choose whichever dress you like. Just ring if you need me to help you find the one that fits best."

"Thank you, Paula. I'm sure at least one will fit me perfectly. I'll be pleased to wear one, especially since Mateo picked them out."

"I'm so happy that Mr. Mateo has found a wonderful woman he wants to marry," she said, smiling again. "We all wondered if he ever would, and if he'd return home. It's…it's a very happy Christmas celebration here at Castillo de Adelaide Fernanda."

Did she really think so? Surely Paula knew Mateo's parents didn't approve of their engagement. But maybe she figured they'd get over it if Mateo came back to live here. The thought made her feel a little sad that everyone in this beautiful house was going to be disappointed that Mateo—the man they'd seen grow up and who was their new heir—wasn't planning to return to his home full-time at all. Unless he thought more about that decision. After walking around the estate with him today, seeing how he felt about the place, she hoped he would.

"Well, thank you again. I'll see you downstairs."

Paula beamed and nodded, leaving Miranda alone, still battling the melancholy she'd felt after her hours with Mateo that afternoon.

Why were family situations often so difficult? Even though he hadn't said much about it, she knew the loss of Mateo's brother had been hard on him. Add to that the stress of his father's health, his parents' demands, and all the people depending on the estate for their livelihoods, and indirectly depending on Mateo, well, she had a feeling he hadn't fully shared the weight he must be carrying around from it all.

No time to dwell on that now. She took a deep breath as she looked at the beautiful dresses neatly hanging in the closet. Ever since she'd become a Davenport, she'd been blessed to be given glamorous clothing like she'd never seen in her life before that. Wearing them to attend various charitable events and symphonies and Broadway shows never got old, she had to admit. But despite having done that now for thirteen years, having these dresses brought here for her to choose from made her feeling absurdly Cinderella-like.

She wished Vanessa was here to see her as the guest and fiancée of a Spanish duke, and couldn't help but enjoy the vision of how her mouth would fall open. Wished Penny was here to see her doing this crazy thing, too, and couldn't wait to tell her about it. Though that reminded her that the adventure would be over and she'd be back to regular old Miranda, living her boring life and working all the time, very soon.

As she flicked through each dress, she couldn't help but imagine which one Mateo would like best. Which one would be the most flattering. Which one would make Mateo look at her the way she caught him doing sometimes. As though he liked what he saw.

The same way she caught herself looking at him.

She drew another deep breath, wishing she could feel totally confident, without worrying which dress would suit her best. But how could she not feel nervous about it, knowing all the guests would be staring at her even before they announced their fake engagement? Feeling curious about the two of them together? Knowing Mateo would be seeing her in a beautiful dress for the very first time, instead of her usual scrubs, or the jeans she'd worn on their excursions?

With her stomach all jittery, she debated the choices in front of her. Should she go with classic black? The shimmery one in pale gold was made of her favorite fabric, a crepe that hung in beautiful folds. Or would the blue one bring out the color of her eyes, which she knew were her best feature? It was probably the one she liked best, so long as it wasn't so low cut that her full figure didn't threaten to fall out of the bodice.

Turning this way and that in front of the full-length mirror, she smiled at the way the cobwebs of blue and aqua threads shimmered as she moved. She eyed the neckline, and decided that, even though her breasts were slightly on display, it wasn't so overt as to be in poor taste, or a reason for people to talk.

The light caught the diamond on her hand, and as she looked at it, melancholy poked at her again. Such a beautiful ring from a beautiful man. Would she ever have someone like him for real?

With a sigh, she grabbed an exquisitely beaded evening bag that had also been provided by her fairy godmother—or in this case, Mateo—and went down the stairs. Nervous butterflies danced in her belly as she wondered how the evening would go; at the same time anticipation welled in her chest at what Mateo would think of how she looked. And what would he look like dressed in his finery? Drool-worthy, without a doubt.

Paula appeared at the base of the stairs, and showed her to the large ballroom where at least three dozen people were already gathered. As she stood in the doorway, her gaze went straight to the most gorgeous man in the room, and her breath caught in her throat.

A perfectly cut tuxedo that had doubtless been tailor made for him enhanced his broad shoulders and regal bearing. One hand held a glass of champagne, the other was tucked in his trouser pocket, elegance and power simply exuding from the man. It struck Miranda that his fellow EMTs would be astounded that the hard-working man usually wearing a uniform and sometimes heavy gear could also look like he'd stepped straight out of a James Bond movie. Calm, capable, and, yes, very, very drool-worthy.

Feeling unable to move, Miranda just stared. She saw him smile and nod to whoever he'd been talking to, then move toward another guest. Maybe he sensed her gawking at him, because he turned and, as their eyes met, she saw him stop dead.

His gaze slowly traveled from her hair to her sparkly shoes, then back up to linger on her breasts before meeting her eyes again. Something about that leisurely perusal made her pulse leap, then flutter even faster as he moved toward her in a relaxed gait that somehow enhanced his graceful sophistication.

When he stopped only inches from her, his hand reached for hers, thumbing the blue diamond ring circling her finger. "You look incredible."

She managed to unstick her tongue from the roof of her mouth. "Thank you. Did you get the dresses because you feared I might wear something to embarrass you?"

"Nothing you could do or wear would ever embarrass me. Even if you wore your hospital scrubs. Though I admit you look even more stunning than you do at work." He smiled, leaning forward to brush his lips against her cheek before speaking softly in her ear. "I know this thing isn't something you've looked forward to. So thank you again for coming. There's not a soul here who won't be dazzled by you."

"You...you look pretty dazzling yourself."

The intimate smile that curved his lips made it hard to breathe, which was further complicated when he closed the small gap between them, pressing his mouth to hers. So softly and sweetly, she closed her eyes and soaked in the sensation, drowned in it, even as the niggle at the back of her mind reminded her he was kissing her to make everyone in the room believe they were in love.

When he drew back, his lips stayed parted, his breath feathering across her moist mouth as their eyes met again. He reached to slide a strand of her hair between his fingers before tucking it behind one ear. "I like your earrings, but I may have to get you blue stones for your ears, too. Of course, your amazing eyes bring the sky into any room you enter."

"There's that romantic, poetic side of you coming out. Who would have guessed?" Her voice was breathy, she knew, but it was the best she could do. The current swirling around them felt like an electrified tornado, holding her close to him.

"Not me. I never knew I had a romantic bent until I met you." He dropped another soft kiss to her mouth. "And speaking of never guessing, who would suspect that Dr. Miranda Davenport was hiding such an incredible body beneath the scrubs she always wears?"

She felt a blush heat her cheeks. "You've seen me out of scrubs."

"Wearing winter street or hiking clothes covering you from neck to toe. Or a thick robe." His voice went lower. "And now I think we should stop talking about seeing you out of scrubs before something happens and I embarrass myself."

The crooked grin he gave her somehow managed to be both amused and sexy at the same time, and she forced herself to look away from it, knowing there had to be a number of people here watching them.

"So, now what? We talk with your parents? Mingle?"

"Both. Then, when we can't take it any more, we dance, so I have an excuse to hold you close."

Miranda swallowed hard, and tried to concentrate on the various people Mateo introduced her to. But it all felt so surreal. Standing beside a handsome, elegant man, wearing a beautiful dress and spectacular engagement ring, with him touching her and looking at her like she meant everything to him. The whole fairy tale come to life.

Except it wasn't. None of it was real, not the flirtatious things he'd said, not the kisses and not the engagement. He was playing the part of loving fiancé for his parents and their guests, and that reality made her throat ache and her chest feel a little hollow.

Stupid. She'd known exactly how this would be, hadn't she? Except she hadn't, not really. All the pretending, knowing Mateo didn't really feel that way about her, made her feel a little empty. Made her ask herself if she'd ever have a man in her life who really did love her.

Somehow she managed to keep her end of the bargain. So many introductions and chit-chat for what seemed like forever left Miranda's cheeks aching. Her smile felt frozen on, especially when talking with Mateo's parents, aunts and uncles.

She'd assumed that Rafael and Ana would at least pretend to be happy about their son's engagement, but it seemed like every time Ana looked her way, she scowled instead of smiled. They hadn't even officially announced it yet, and now it seemed that they really might not, probably to give Mateo more time to think about it, as they'd said yesterday. Though it was obvious people had figured it out, as she'd seen and heard the whispers about Mateo's future wife.

Miranda knew she shouldn't be bothered by his parents' attitude. She should try to understand that they were hurting horribly over their son's death, and because of that weren't able to think in a normal way right now. Except Mateo had told her they'd always favored his brother and, watching their distant and cool treatment of him, it was sadly easy to believe.

"Mateo! My handsome brother-in-law. It's been far too long since you've come home."

Miranda knew it was wrong to instantly judge the small blonde with an obviously saccharine smile as she hugged Mateo, giving him the European two-cheek kiss as she did so. Except how could she not? She'd been prejudiced by what Mateo, and Paula, too, had told her about the woman who was obviously his brother Emilio's widow.

"Hello, Camilla." Mateo quickly extricated himself from her grasp and turned to Miranda. She couldn't help but feel impressed at his impassive expression. She knew how he felt about Emilio's wife, but no one would know it. For the first time that night, he introduced her as his fiancée, despite his parents not having made any announcement, and Miranda wondered if it was to keep the woman from making a play for him, as he'd said she'd done in the past.

"Well, well. The woman who finally reined in Mateo Alves. I didn't think I'd ever see the day. It's so very good to meet you." Camilla smiled brightly, but her eyes were even colder than Mateo's mother's, and held something else besides disapproval.

Disdain? Jealousy? Miranda had no idea, but she did know that she disliked the woman instantly.

"Nice to meet you, too." If only to see that Mateo wasn't making things up about the woman. The way she looked at Mateo, then Miranda, showed loud and clear how she felt about him belonging to someone else. Was she the kind of woman who wanted any man she could claim, or did she have a real thing for her late husband's brother?

"When is the big, happy day?"

"We're still finalizing our plans. But don't worry, I'm sure my mother will apprise you of it as soon as we decide." Mateo's arm tightened around Miranda's waist, but his cordial expression didn't change.

"I'm glad to see you're finally stepping up to your duty to your parents. Emilio felt so frustrated, hurt really, that you never came to help."

Miranda cringed at the woman's nasty barb, knowing that had to score a painful, direct hit on Mateo. She glanced up at him, and the tic in his jaw and tightness of his lips showed she was right.

"I don't think I'm the one who hurt him. But do I wish I'd been here for him when things got rough? Yeah. I regret that more than you'll ever know."

He swung away with Miranda still held in the crook of his arm and strode toward the dance floor. She thought about saying something about his exchange with Camilla, but his hard, fierce expression told her that keeping quiet was a better choice.

A headache began to form in both temples, and just as she was considering telling Mateo she'd like to excuse herself for a while he led her onto the dance floor. His arm stayed closed around her as he grasped her hand, but he didn't pull her close. Probably, he was as exhausted by the charade as she was.

"How are you holding up?"

"I was about to ask you the same thing."

"Don't worry about me." The tension around his eyes and in his jaw had her wanting to reach up to somehow smooth it away. "I'm used to people whispering and talking about me. About why I moved away. About why I don't come home often. Bringing you here has greased the gossip wheel, doubtless making everyone's day as they wonder what's going on."

No mention of Camilla and her words. "It doesn't bother you that your parents obviously aren't going to announce our...our engagement?"

He shrugged as he swept her into a turn. "My goal with our engagement was to buy some time. Give my parents a reason to understand why I'm not coming back full-time. We've accomplished that goal, so I don't care about the rest."

She wished she could say the same. Stupid as it was, there was still that tiny part of her that felt a little like she had as a teenager showing up at the Davenport home, barely tolerated by the matriarch.

Another turn took them to the edge of the room, and to her surprise Mateo swept them out the French doors onto a wide stone loggia dimly lit by the lights from the ballroom. The cool air felt good against her cheeks, and it felt wonderful to be away from the crowded room.

They came to a stop next to a wide pillar, and Mateo tipped her chin up, their eyes meeting.

"You didn't answer my earlier question."

"What question?"

"About how you were holding up. Is it bothering you that people are talking about you? That my parents have virtually ignored you?"

She nearly denied it, not wanting him to worry about something so silly when they weren't really a couple. But the brown eyes looking into hers seemed to already see what she was feeling. "It shouldn't, I know. But I can't help feeling a little…uncomfortable about it, you know?"

"I know. After what you told me about your lack of welcome by Vanessa Davenport, I've been worried. I wouldn't have asked you to do this if I'd known. I'm sorry."

"No need to be sorry. Honestly." He looked so concerned, she tried to reassure him. "It's just baggage that I shouldn't still be carrying around with me."

"There's no 'should' or 'shouldn't' when it comes to feelings, Miranda," he said quietly. "We feel how we feel."

She stared up at him, seeing that was true for

both of them. And it struck her that observing the way Mateo was dealing with tough issues and feelings of grief and loss had made her think about her own life and how she'd been living it. While all the flirting and kissing didn't mean anything, his confidence in her did. And maybe that meant it was long past the time she should learn to have more confidence in herself.

"I know. But maybe what we're feeling isn't based on reality. Vanessa didn't want me around, but it didn't take long for everyone else to accept me. Maybe it's time I accept myself."

"What about yourself haven't you accepted?"

"That I don't have to keep pushing myself to try to live up to the Davenport name. Maybe I've accomplished that."

"No maybe about it." He tugged her closer. "You're a very special woman in a beautiful, tempting package."

The warm rumble of his voice, the way he was looking at her, sent her thoughts away from her past and her lack of confidence. They made her think about him, and that he was right. That how she felt wasn't something she could control, which was a deep attraction and connection to this man. Could he have been thinking that, too, when he'd talked about feeling what they felt? Was there any way his kisses and touches were more than a show of make-believe?

"I guess that's true," she whispered. She licked her lips, wanting more than anything to kiss him, to explore those feelings squeezing her chest and heating her body even in the crisp November air. But what if that's not what he'd meant at all? What if she embarrassed him, and herself, which would just complicate an already odd situation? What if putting herself at risk like that would be a huge mistake?

Wearing her high heels, his mouth was at her eye level, and she found herself fixated on the shape of it, thinking of how it felt to kiss him, and her own lips involuntarily parted. Heat curled in her belly, and that swirling electricity seemed to charge the air around them all over again. She managed to lift her gaze to his, and the eyes that met hers held a hot flicker of awareness that sent her pulse racing.

His hands tightened on her arms, bringing her close. The slight tic showed in his jaw again, and his eyes slid to her mouth, but he didn't move to kiss her.

She pressed her palms against his hard chest. Feeling the heavy beat of his heart, she suddenly decided to go for it. To use her new-found confidence. To find out exactly what he might be feeling—hadn't doing crazy things been part of her reason to come here?

"So what are you feeling right now?" she

asked. Before he had a chance to answer, she shocked herself, finding she couldn't wait to hear his response, sliding her hands up around his neck to kiss him. For a split second his mouth stayed soft until, with a soft groan, he kissed her back. Taking it deeper, hotter, sliding one hand up her back to tangle his fingers in her hair.

Her body melted against his, the kiss spreading fire across her skin and weakening her knees. When his lips separated an inch from hers, she looked up into hungry eyes gone black, both of them breathless.

"What I'm feeling is obvious, isn't it?" he said in a low rumble. "I think you know that I want you, Miranda. That I'm attracted to you in a way I don't remember feeling before. But I can't offer you what you want and need in your life. And it wouldn't be fair to take advantage of you after I've brought you nearly captive into this ruse."

"I'm not captive. And I'm not asking for anything other than for you to kiss me. Unless even that's more than you're willing to offer."

A slow smile curved his lips, even as he looked at her like getting her naked was suddenly all he wanted. "As you've already noticed, kissing you any time, any place, has always been high on my list of offerings, *mi belleza*."

His lips caressed her jaw, moved to the sensitive spot beneath her ear, sending a delicious shiver down her spine. Slowly traveling down her neck, his hot mouth kept going until they rested on the mounds exposed there, his tongue leisurely licking along her neckline making her gasp.

"Your breasts tantalize me, Miranda." His breath whispered across the dampness of her skin. "So beautiful, so soft."

She clutched the back of his head, loving the way he nuzzled the cleft between her breasts, nearly hyperventilating with the sensation of it as his hands moved to her hips and over her buttocks.

"Mateo! Mateo, where are you?"

The distant voice permeated the sexual fog clogging her brain. Miranda opened her eyes as he lifted his head, his eyes glittering into hers. "Shh." He pressed his lips to hers. "My mother. Probably someone important in her world has arrived and she wants me to talk to them. If we're lucky, she won't look out here."

"She'll think even less of me if I'm keeping you away from her guests."

"And you care because?"

Just as they were smiling at one another, his mother's voice calling him got louder, frantic sounding, and Mateo straightened to his full height, a frown dipping between his brows as his arms fell to his sides. "I'd better go and see what's wrong. I'll be back."

"I'll come with you."

In her heels, Miranda couldn't keep up with him as he strode through the ballroom, all the guests moving to make way for him. Across the room, she could see his mother leaning over a large, wingback chair and in it sat Mateo's father, slumped to one side, looking extremely ill.

CHAPTER TEN

"MOVE BACK, PLEASE. Mother, give us some room." Fear tightened Mateo's chest, but he ignored it as best he could, relying on his medical training to address the problem, without letting emotion cloud his perspective. This wouldn't be the first time his father's Parkinson's disease had left the poor man feeling weak and out of it, but it was always alarming, no matter how much they'd all become somewhat used to it.

Mateo crouched next to his father's chair, concentrating on getting his pulse. Trying hard to ignore the way his head was lolled back and the gibberish and strange sentences he was stringing together in a slurred voice that constricted Mateo's gut even more.

"When did he start to feel this way?"

"I'm not sure." His mother stood to the side, clutching her hands together. "I was talking with guests, and haven't been with him for a while. But he was having a bad day to begin with. Felt extra-shaky this morning and couldn't sit very straight. He was feeling anxious about that, with our guests coming tonight."

"What's his pulse?"

Miranda asked the question in a quiet voice as she crouched beside him. He glanced up to see that piercing blue carefully studying his father. "Bradycardia—about fifty. Some arrhythmia."

Sweat prickled his body as he turned back to his father, feeling uneasy about the way he was staring at him, barely blinking. "I think we should get him to bed and give him a dose of his medications. Usually when he's having a bad day, that helps."

"The horses!" Rafael suddenly exclaimed, shakily waving his hand. "There! Don't let them in the house!"

God, he hated that this terrible disease was slowly whittling away at the strong man his father had always been. No matter how many times he experienced it, his father suffering hallucinations because of his disease deeply disturbed Mateo, and his mother, too, and he sucked in a breath, forcing himself to respond in a matter-of-fact tone.

"No horses here, Padre. They're all safe in the stable. Let's get you to bed so you can rest, okay?"

"No! Not leaving." His father was shouting

now, looking a little wild-eyed and mulish. "We're waiting for Emilio to get here."

Emilio. Mateo's chest squeezed, wishing with all his heart that could be true. "Emilio's not coming, Father, so you don't need to wait. Let's go so you can get a little rest now." He pinned his gaze on his mother with a message he hoped she read loud and clear. "Get the staff to clear the room. You know he wouldn't want this kind of audience."

She stared at him before jerkily nodding. Instantly, she instructed the staff to move the food to another room, and asked the guests to follow.

"Didn't you say he's diabetic, too?" Miranda asked, a frown dipping deep between her brows. "We should check his blood sugar before you take him to his room. Where is his glucose meter?"

Mateo glanced at her, surprised. "It's not uncommon for his Parkinson's symptoms to flare up sometimes. A decreased blink rate and hallucinations are all part of that."

"I understand. But shakiness, delirium, and belligerence are all symptoms of hypoglycemia, too, which you know."

Well, damn. Because his father's Parkinson's was such a big concern, both he and his mother had assumed he was just having a bad day. But could Miranda be right? "Paula, can you please get Father's glucose monitor?"

"You think this might be his diabetes?" His mother looked anxiously at Mateo, then her gaze slid to Miranda.

"Not sure. Do you know what he's eaten today?"

"I don't know. We were all busy with the party, and I didn't pay attention like I usually do. Perhaps he didn't…" She stopped talking and turned, obviously distraught, to one of the staff who'd been tending the buffet. "Please bring some food right away."

"Not yet," Miranda said gently, reaching for her hand to try to calm her down. "If it's hypo-glycemia, he could easily choke, trying to eat."

His mother stared at Miranda, then nodded as she gripped her hand. "Then what…?"

"We need some regular, granulated sugar, please," Miranda said. "As soon as possible."

"Yes. Do as the doctor says. Right away."

The staff member rushed off, and Miranda wrapped her arm around Ana's shoulders to give her a reassuring hug. The respect in her eyes as she looked at Miranda was beyond good to see. Much as Mateo hated seeing his father feeling so ill and unsteady, maybe the silver lining would be new respect for his pretend bride-to-be.

Paula rushed in with the glucose monitor, and he quickly pricked his father's finger to draw the drop of blood they needed, his father now practically bellowing in protest, yanking his hand back, making it harder to get the test strip in place. In moments, though, the test showed exactly what Miranda had obviously expected.

An extremely low reading practically screamed from the monitor. Miranda's gaze lifted from the test at the same time his did. Their eyes met, and he gave her a smile and a nodding salute.

"Miranda was right. His blood sugar is very low, Mother."

"Oh, dear. This is terrible." She wrung her hands, looking nearly ready to cry. "This is my fault for not attending to him."

"It's not your fault." Mateo reached for her tense hands again, giving them a reassuring squeeze. "We need to set up a system where others in the house are also paying attention to his meals from now on. It isn't fair to you to feel you have to hover over him every time he's supposed to eat, and be the only one checking his blood sugar."

"Thank God you were here to help. To find what was wrong."

His gut clenched at the tears that sprang into his mother's eyes. That she was right made his chest ache. Made him wonder if he could let himself make the same mistake with his parents that he'd made with Emilio. In not being here for him when his brother had needed him most.

He rubbed his hand across his forehead and looked away from his mother's distress. What was he going to do about this complicated problem?

He drew a deep breath before turning back to his mother, explaining what needed to happen now. At the same time, Miranda went to work. He knew it definitely wasn't the way she'd normally take care of hypoglycemia in the hospital. But had he really said in the tunnel that she didn't know anything about field medicine? Her simple but efficient treatment showed he'd been wrong about that as he watched her stick her finger straight into the sugar bowl she'd been given and wipe it directly onto his father's tongue.

She talked soothingly as she slathered on another teaspoon-sized dollop of sugar, his father no longer protesting but making little smacking sounds as he swallowed. His eyes began to focus and blink more when he stared up at Miranda and Mateo, obviously slowly becoming more alert, though at the same time he clearly was confused by what was going on.

"Feeling a little better?" Miranda asked with a smile.

"What...? I don't... Why?"

"It's all right, Father." Mateo reached for his father's thin hand. "You can't have eaten much today, and got into a little trouble because of that.

But your blood sugar is coming up now. You're going to be okay."

His father nodded, obviously feeling a little wiped out, which was hardly a surprise. Mateo stood, helping Miranda up to stand next to him. He kept his arm around her waist as he spoke to his mother, then ordered some food brought to his father. His mother insisted on sitting next to him, poking food into his mouth, and Mateo knew it was because she didn't trust anyone else to do it, feeling guilty that he'd gotten into trouble to begin with.

With everything settled, he finally could turn to look at Miranda's beautiful smile, and he knew it wasn't just gratitude that filled his chest with an overwhelming emotion. The chatter and dishes clanking around them faded as he looked into her warm blue eyes, felt how perfectly her body fit in his arm, and it seemed as though the world was turning on its axis. His breath backed up in his lungs as the truth smacked him square in the solar plexus. As he realized that what he was feeling for Miranda was something he'd never experienced before.

He was teetering dangerously close to loving this amazing woman. He wanted to pull her close and kiss her, but wasn't sure if he should let himself do that. Though he had a feeling there was no way he could resist, since he sure as hell hadn't managed to keep his distance so far. Except she deserved so much more than a man like him, and he battled back the urge to tell her exactly how he was feeling.

The quizzical expression on her face as she looked at him had him wondering what his face looked like, and he swallowed hard, still reeling from his revelation.

"Are you okay?"

He nodded, having no idea if he was okay or not, then somehow managed to speak. "Thank you. You just might have saved my father's life tonight."

Her face went pink. "You would have figured it out."

"Maybe not in time to prevent him from going into a coma. Having experienced my father's Parkinson's symptoms so many times, I was being tunnel-visioned, assuming that was what was happening."

"Easy to do when you're as close to it as you are. I had the advantage of being an impartial observer."

"And an excellent doctor."

"Like you said before, we make a good team."

"Yeah, we really do." The truth of that shocked him. When was the last time he'd felt that way? Once he'd left the army, he'd mostly isolated himself, except when he'd worked on patients with other EMTs. But the more time he spent with Miranda, the more he realized what a truly special woman she was, in so many ways. A woman he was falling way too hard for.

He leaned down to give her a soft kiss, wishing they could go back to what they'd been doing before, which had involved having his lips and tongue kissing her and caressing her beautiful breasts. "I'm going to help my father to his room and keep an eye on him for a little while. I'll find you later?"

"I'll be here."

She'd be there. His chest filled again with a mix of emotions at her words. He knew it was true. Knew that she'd be there for him because that was the kind of woman she was, and he'd never needed her more than at this moment. And yet it was also a reminder that he hadn't done the same for his brother, which was a terrible regret he somehow had to learn to live with.

"Gracias," he said, his voice rough. "I'll see you as soon as I can. And, *mi belleza*? Please plan for us to take up right where we left off."

Each time she walked along the stone paths meandering through the back gardens of the Alves estate, Miranda found it a little more peaceful. The fingernail moon still hung within a thin mist of clouds, surrounded by the kind of twinkling stars she rarely got to see back in the city. The night sky of New York City was lit by millions of city lights, not nature and the universe, and this sight made her heart feel a calmness and serenity she hadn't felt since…well, she couldn't remember ever feeling quite this way.

Mateo had told her the gardens had been there for hundreds of years, carefully tended and refurbished as necessary, full of gorgeous blooms of all kinds during the spring and summer months. She found herself wishing she could see it during other seasons, instead of dormant as it was in November. Found herself wishing she could spend more time with Mateo, too.

Neither of those was going to happen. Yes, he'd said he wanted to take up where they'd left off an hour or so ago, and just the thought made her feel flushed and breathless. He might have kissed her because he'd wanted to, because he'd wanted *her*, as he'd so excitingly told her, and not because he was trying to convince everyone that their fake engagement was real. But kissing her now, wanting her tonight and for as long as they were here together was a far cry from wanting a relationship once they were back in the city.

He'd stated very clearly that he wasn't interested in a long-term relationship with any woman. And she wanted the loving husband her mother had never had, wanted to be blessed with children. A close-knit family that was all her own, that no one could ever take away from her. But did that rule out a simple but doubtless glorious fling with Mateo?

A deep sigh left her lungs. Feeling confused and unsettled by the question, she looked up at the stars for guidance. "Star light, star bright, what do you think I should wish for tonight?" she asked aloud.

"If you don't already know, why are you here with my son?"

Startled, Miranda's hand flew to her chest as she swung toward the voice to see Ana walking toward her. "I'm sorry, I didn't know you were out here."

"I'm glad we have this time to talk privately. First, I wish to thank you for your help with my husband tonight."

Relaxing a little, Miranda smiled. "I became an ER doctor to help others, so I'm glad I could be of assistance."

Ana inclined her head, and as she moved closer, Miranda's smile faded. The woman might have slightly thawed with her thanks, and her expression might not be cold any more, but it was weary rather than warm.

"I appreciate it more than I can express. But, despite that, you must know that neither my husband nor I will ever give our blessing to a wedding between you and our son."

And there it was all over again. It shouldn't feel like she'd been stabbed in the chest with a sharp instrument, since it wasn't exactly news that the Alveses didn't approve of her, but it felt like that anyway. "Why not?"

"I have tried to help you and Mateo understand, but neither of you seem to be listening. With the death of our special Emilio…" Her voice hitched for a moment before she continued, "Mateo must take over his role as the heir to the dukedom. And you cannot fill the role of his wife."

"Why not?" Miranda repeated, somewhat stupidly. Why was she even asking, when their engagement wasn't real anyway? Did she want all the reasons she didn't fit in spelled out in capital letters to make her feel inadequate, like a lesser human being, just like she had thirteen years ago?

"Because you are American, and have an important job there. We are so very afraid that if he marries you, he'll never come back." She reached to clutch Miranda's hands. "We need him to marry a Spaniard, someone who will be content, happy to live here at the Castillo de Adelaide Fernanda. Surely seeing how ill my husband was tonight shows you how much Mateo is needed here, especially since…since Emilio left us. I can't bear to lose both my sons."

Miranda's heart squeezed at the pain and fear in Ana's eyes. "Mateo does understand." Miranda chose her words carefully, not wanting to speak for Mateo but wanting to pass on basically what he'd told her. "Our being together does mean he'll be living in New York part of the time, but he expects to come here several times a year."

"That's not enough. We need him here, which is why you must let him go." She reached to touch Miranda's arm, an imploring expression on her tired face. "You met my Emilio's wife tonight. You saw what a wonderful woman she is. A woman who adored her husband. My son." She lifted her wrist, encircled with a glittering gold bracelet studded with pearls. "Emilio gave this to me when he first took over running the estate, on my birthday. A gift to show me his commitment to me and our family and his responsibilities. Camilla helped him choose it, I know. She's a woman full of grace and style, loving and giving and from a good family with deep roots here. She has told me she will help find a suitable wife for Mateo."

Astonishment, anger, and hurt burned in Miranda's chest. Even if Mateo hadn't told her the truth about his sister-in-law, she'd have been upset at Ana's utterly rude dismissal of *her* as being worthy in any way of her second son.

"What makes you think I don't adore your other son the way you believe Camilla adored Emilio? And why would he want to marry someone who doesn't love him? Perhaps your attitude is why Mateo doesn't want to come back here to live and work full-time."

"What do you mean? I love my son more than anything in the world. A wild boy as a child, we knew the army would bring him focus, and his many medals prove that it did. He's a fine man now, and I have to believe he will step up to his duties as the heir."

"Have you tried to talk to him about all this? About his plans? Maybe his answers would surprise you."

"The only surprise has been his engagement to you, which is the one thing that would keep him away. I would guess that once you found out Mateo wasn't like other emergency medical professionals in the U.S., but, in fact, a wealthy man from a family whose dukedom goes back hundreds of years, you set your net out to snag him as quickly as possible. It's what too many women do."

Miranda gasped in disbelief, anger surging so fast into her skull it made her brain scorch. "I can't believe you would actually say such a thing when you don't know me at all." She wanted to talk about her own family's wealth, her personal hardships, her hard work to prove herself to everyone, but decided she wouldn't stoop to the other woman's arrogant and judgmental depths. But she couldn't keep from telling her, at least when it came to the money, how wrong she was.

"For your information, it's been my experience that fortune hunters impressed by pedigree and money are often represented by the male sex, disguised as appreciative suitors. I've been targeted by fortune hunters interested in everything but me personally since I was in high school. Believe me, the absolutely last reason I'm attracted to Mateo is his money and position here, and the expectations you carry for him as the next Duke. In fact, that's the only thing I can think of that would make me walk away."

She spun away, the woman's words clawing at her gut, her own words disturbing her in a different way.

The only thing that would make her walk away was his parents' attitude?

As she nearly ran back to the house, her breathing went haywire at the realization that, deep inside, she'd meant it. And what did that mean, when all this had begun as a charade? A planned strategy by Mateo, with some pleasant vacation time in the midst of it?

She clutched her coat close to her throat, a

stark and scary reality slamming into her, making it hard to breathe.

What had started out as pretence had become horrifyingly real for her. Somehow she'd let herself fall hard for Mateo Alves. A man who had no interest in a real and lasting relationship with any woman.

She dropped onto one of the outdoor chairs on the loggia and clutched her cold hands together. Mateo had wanted a simple excuse to bide his time taking on his family duties, and have them eventually accept that he wouldn't live here full-time. She'd wanted to help him with that, not fully understanding the difficult dynamics of his family situation after his brother's death.

Now she did. His parents' pain over losing their son was still raw. And even though he hadn't said much about it, she knew Mateo's was, too. No one thought clearly during times of grief. If she was truly a friend to Mateo, she'd help him see that all of them needed more time to process it, to figure out what needed to happen next.

Maybe Mateo really should move back here for a while. Ease his parents' fears. Studying psychology was part of medical school, and she had to assume that the reason Ana had lashed out at her with such harsh words was because, deep inside, she felt scared to death. Her husband was ill, and would slowly get worse with time.

She'd lost her beloved son who'd been there to support her. She didn't realize that she'd driven her other son away once, and was doing it again.

As she thought it through, trying hard to see it from Ana's perspective, Miranda's heart felt heavy, hurting for Mateo and for all of them. Because to make one of them happy, the other would be unhappy. So where did that leave them?

She didn't know, but what she did know? She'd lived that quandary herself. Being able to leave behind poverty and an uncertain future to become part of the Davenport family, eventually becoming close to her half-siblings, meant Vanessa had had to endure seeing the physical reminder of her husband's infidelity every single day. Vanessa being happy instead would have left Miranda in a very dark and hopeless place.

A shadowy figure emerged from the garden, and she looked up to see Ana moving up the ancient stone steps to stand next to her, her face now filled with worry instead of hostility.

"I am sorry to have insulted you by assuming you are after money and prestige. Maybe you genuinely care for Mateo. But you must see why we need him here, where he belongs, while you have your work and your own family back where you belong. Do you understand?"

"I believe I do." She rose and let herself really see the pain and anxiety in the woman's eyes.

Seeing it there forced her to really look at what a tough situation the Alves family was in. And because she wasn't a part of it, not for real, she suddenly knew it was time for her to go. To let Mateo and his parents work out this problem for themselves, without her being there to muddy everything up with a relationship and engagement that wasn't even real. Her being here, participating in this charade, was just making things worse. Making it impossible for Mateo to stay longer, to deal with the pain of Emilio's death together with his parents. To mend the fences between them.

"I'll be going now," she said quietly. "I'll ask Mateo to cut our trip short so I can go back to New York. Let him decide if he's coming back with me now or staying longer as you...talk more about everything."

A tremulous smile formed on Ana's lips. "Thank you. With you breaking off your engagement, I know Mateo will—"

"Breaking off our engagement?"

Both women swung toward the French doors to see a frowning Mateo striding toward them.

CHAPTER ELEVEN

"WHAT'S GOING ON out here?" Mateo asked. "I was trying to find you, to tell you that Father is feeling much better, only to hear my fiancée is leaving me?" He folded his arms across his chest, giving his mother a sharp look. "What are you talking about? What have you said to her?"

"Merely what you already know, and that she now understands." His mother lifted her chin defiantly. "You must think about your family and why we need you here, without an engagement complicating your thoughts and decisions."

"My decisions are exactly that—mine! Why do you refuse to accept that?"

"Because you know there's more at stake here than selfishly pandering to your own desires! What has happened to you? You spent four years in the army, defending our country and our way of life, always living up to your responsibilities. How has that changed now that you're needed here more than ever?"

"I like my life in New York. I still see no reason why I can't take care of the responsibilities you speak of while living here only part of the year."

"Your brother worked hard here, many hours a week, managing all the business interests of the estate. That's not something that can be done part-time, or from across the ocean." His mother stepped close to him and glared. "You know that Camilla was the perfect wife for Emilio. Glamorous and conscientious, the perfect hostess. You can't choose a mate who has significant work, like being a doctor. A career that would make those other important obligations impossible to meet. Surely you see that!"

"What I see is a woman who refuses to open her eyes to the truth." Mateo's voice vibrated with anger. "Camilla made Emilio miserable! And that's the kind of woman you would choose again for your other son? Camilla hurt my brother over and over again with her infidelity, having numerous affairs with all kinds of men, from politicians to horse trainers to men with trust funds who care only for their jet-setting lifestyle."

Ana gasped. "That is not true!"

"It is true. Why do you think he got so reckless? Began base jumping from places he shouldn't, and went paragliding on a day he *knew* was dangerously windy, only to be killed because of it!"

"It...it was just a terrible accident!"

"Yes, but he knew that mountain like the back of his hand, and I'm as sure as I am of my own name that it was one of Camilla's hurtful affairs that filled him with the desperate need to go out paragliding on a day he knew he shouldn't. He needed the escape from pain that paragliding always gave both of us. You pushed Emilio into a terrible marriage, just as you're trying to push me to be who you want me to be. But I won't accept that. I want the freedom to choose the life I want with the woman I love, and that woman is Miranda!" He moved away from his mother, tugging Miranda up from her seat to hold her close against his side. "We will be leaving tomorrow morning. I'll be in touch from New York."

And with that he marched back into the house, taking Miranda with him. Her heart pounded hard in her chest from the tense exchange and confusion from his words.

Of course he'd just been angry and upset. He didn't mean what he'd said about her being the woman he loved. She knew that. And yet there'd been something about the way he'd said it—something about the timbre of his voice and the look in his eyes when he'd wrapped his arm around her that seemed to say he had meant it.

Could that be possible? Could he really have come to care for her the way she had for him, even though they'd spent mere days together? Surely that was just wishful thinking on her part.

"I'm so sorry, Miranda," he said through gritted teeth as he led her through the house. "I would never have brought you here if I'd known how bad it would be for you. And even after you diagnosed my father's hypoglycemia and took care of him! My mother should be ashamed."

"She's suffering, Mateo." Miranda wrapped her arm around his waist and gave it a squeeze as they walked side by side toward the stairs leading to the room where she'd changed into her gown. "I've been thinking about how hard all this must be for her, how scary to feel somewhat alone now. Your father is sick and you all know the prognosis for his future is grim. She's lost a son that she loved."

"And I lost a brother that I loved. That's not an excuse to act horribly to someone."

"People do and say things in times of deep stress that they might not otherwise," she said quietly.

He came to a stop. "You amaze me." He grasped her shoulders and pulled her hard against him, his eyes still angry but looking at her searchingly, too. "Another example of how sweet and special and wonderful you are. Trying to understand and forgive someone who's treated you badly, instead of feeling angry and resentful. You did it with

Vanessa, too, and your father. It's just one more reason why I've come to love you."

Her heart felt like it stopped beating completely. She stared up at him, trying to see if he truly meant the words that seemed impossible. Impossibly wonderful. Had he said it just because he was feeling emotional? Upset with his mother and with the situation he faced?

"Love me?"

"Yes, love you." He kissed her long and hard, and through it she could feel a passion that made her legs wobble, tightly interwoven with clear anger and distress. "I want our engagement to be real, Miranda. I want to make a life with you in New York, far away from here and my parents."

"Mateo, you...you don't mean that." Miranda's chest constricted so hard she couldn't breathe. "You're just feeling frustrated with everything, and will feel different tomorrow when you've got a little distance from your mother to understand her better."

"I do mean it. And there's something that *you* don't understand." His hands gripped her shoulders. "I told you that my parents never thought highly of me, the way they did Emilio. But now that I'm all they've got, suddenly they want me to come home. If I come back here for good, I'll be surrounded by the knowledge, every day, that

I'm not good enough to take his place. I'm just not. I never have been."

"Of course you are," she protested, finding it unimaginable that he seemed to truly believe it. "Why do you say that?"

"Because I've never been the son to them that Emilio was. I wasn't here for my brother when he needed me most." He pressed his mouth to hers for another hard kiss. "I know I don't deserve you, but for the first time in my life I want to share it with someone. Share it with you. For-ever."

Oh, God. She wanted to believe it. So much. She searched his eyes, trying to figure out what was really happening here. To see if tomorrow he'd regret his declaration of love, his claim that he wanted a forever-after with her. What she saw in their dark, smoldering depths sent cautious joy surging to her heart.

Heat. Shimmering desire. And the same glow of love that had slowly, insistently crept into every pore, every inch of her being over the past few days.

"I don't know what to think," she whispered. "I don't know what to say."

"Then let me show you how I'm feeling. Let me take you back to the guest house and con-vince you I mean every word."

He moved toward a side door that led into the

dark night, heading quickly toward the small house as the stars twinkled above them.

Gulping in the crisp air, excitement surged through Miranda's veins, and her stomach flipped inside out. "Show" her how he was feeling? That could only mean one thing, couldn't it?

He pushed open the front door and, seeming like he was in a hurry, backed her into the bedroom and kicked the door closed behind them. "I don't expect Paula or anyone to show up, but just in case, hmm?"

The hard edge of anger had left his voice. The low rumble that replaced it was so full of seduction and promise, Miranda trembled in anticipation. He shoved off the coat she hadn't even noticed she was still wearing and tossed it on a chair before turning her around. His warm fingers swept her hair from the back of her neck and she felt his lips follow, pressing tiny kisses to her nape as he unzipped the beautiful dress.

"Mateo…" She had no idea what to say after his name, but even if she had, all ability to speak disappeared as cool air slipped across her bare back inch by inch, his fingers following in a shivery path across her skin. Finally fully unzipped, his hands gently shoved the dress to the floor with a swish. His lips moved to her bare shoulders as he turned her to face him again, his dark eyes glittering as he slowly, excruciatingly ran his finger along the lacy top of her bra.

Part of her wanted him to just keep going, but she didn't want to be the only one standing there in her underwear. She reached for his bowtie and gave it a tug, sliding it from his collar to drop on the floor before reaching for his shirt. Struggling with the small buttons, she couldn't help making a frustrated noise, and with a heated smile he swept her hands aside.

"Let me."

"All right," she breathed. "That leaves me free to work on the rest of your clothes."

Another chuckle morphed abruptly into a moan as she quickly loosened his belt, undid his pants, pushed them to his ankles, then pressed the palm of her hand to feel the hard erection tenting his underwear.

"*Dio mio*. Slow down." He kicked his pants legs off at the same time he yanked off his shirt. "We have all night."

"I'm feeling in a hurry." And, wow, was that ever true. All worries about how he truly felt about her were forgotten as, with the sexiest smile she'd ever seen, he drew her close and kissed her. First on her mouth then her cheeks and throat then back to her mouth, speaking melodic Spanish words between each one, until she was gasping and clutching his bare shoulders to keep from slithering to the floor.

His hands had tantalizingly stroked and caressed her skin as they'd kissed, exploring her shoulder blades, her hips, her ribs, until one finally moved to unhook her bra, and he drew it off to toss it somewhere. His hands lifted to cup her breasts, his thumbs sliding softly across her nipples.

He lifted his fathomless dark gaze to hers. "You have the most beautiful breasts I've ever seen," he whispered. "Ever touched. Ever kissed." He lowered his hot mouth and slowly ran his tongue over each mound and Miranda held him close, resting her cheek against his soft hair, amazed at the intense connection she felt with this man after mere days spent together.

In a sudden, swift scoop he lifted her against his chest, her breasts being teased this time by the soft rasp of his chest hair as he pressed her against him. He moved to the bed, pulled back the quilt and laid her on the cool sheets, quickly following to lie on her, kiss her and touch her. The heavy weight of him felt so good, so right, and when he slid his fingers down to caress her she gasped into his mouth. He responded with sweet-sounding Spanish words, repeating them over and over as he pushed her thighs farther apart, touching, teasing, until she couldn't bear it any longer.

"I need you inside me now," she gasped.

"I'm here to give you whatever you want, my beautiful one," he whispered. "Always." He rose up to slowly fill her, and her legs wrapped around his back to pull him as close as two people could possibly be.

"Mateo. Mateo. I feel so… It's so…" She found she couldn't say anything more, just moaned at the bliss building inside her as he moved, deep and slow and unbearably delicious.

"I know, *querida*," he said, his gaze locked passionately with hers. "For me, too."

They moved together in a perfect rhythm that built, grew faster and faster until she couldn't hold back the intense pleasure any longer. She cried out as she came, feeling Mateo follow her with a deep groan of his own, until they lay gasping against one another, unable to move.

Long minutes later Mateo lifted his head. The dark eyes staring into hers seemed to hold a deep seriousness, but at the same time a small smile curved his lips. "Miranda Davenport, I love you."

"I love you too," she whispered.

"Finally!" His smile widened. "Hearing you say it back shows me you finally believe I love you. Took you long enough."

Her heart squeezed with an overflowing

bubble of happiness. Until something sharply stabbed to deflate that joy.

Disquiet.

Did she believe him? She wanted to. So much. Yet a niggling doubt told her again that it seemed sudden. Too sudden. Right on the heels of the stress of the whole visit, of time spent in the orchards and seeing the horses, of his dad getting ill, of arguing with his mother. Of coping with his brother's death. Of dealing with his obviously deep-rooted feelings of inadequacy when it came to his place in the family.

Spending time together in Catalonia and on the estate had been a pleasant distraction from the weight of all that. Great sex was the perfect way to ease pain, she knew. Was he confusing all those feelings with love?

God, she just didn't know. The chemistry between them from the very beginning, the feelings they'd seemed to share at the dance, wasn't necessarily love on his part. Maybe it was simple chemistry. Lust.

Except surely a man like Mateo knew the difference between lust and love. Much as she wanted to believe with all her heart that he really did love her, she had to question it. Had to wonder.

Did he truly believe it himself?

* * *

Mateo held tight to Miranda's gloved hand as they navigated the crowded sidewalks on their way to his apartment. They'd enjoyed another dinner together, talking and laughing and learning about one another, and every hour he spent with her, the more he appreciated her. Her pretty face and beautiful smile, her inquisitive mind, her insight into so many things he didn't usually bother to spend much time thinking about.

He hated that they both had to go back to work the next day, since their vacation time had been far less than satisfying. Had hardly counted as a vacation at all, with all the stress of faking their engagement and dealing with his parents.

She'd protested that he should think about it longer, but he was more than glad they'd left early the next morning. Once they'd arrived back home, they'd spent their last days off going to a few museums he hadn't taken the time to go to recently, to a show, even ice skating at the Rockefeller Center. Laughing as they both fell a few times, enjoying the beauty and magic of Christmastime in New York City.

And making love. Making love with Miranda was like nothing he'd experienced before, probably because he'd never really loved a woman before. How incredible that this woman he'd planned to spend only one week with had sneaked into his heart so completely. Turning upside down his conviction that he never wanted to be committed to one woman, because he knew without a doubt that he wanted to spend his life with her.

He smiled down at her, tugging her away from a gaggle of laughing teenagers dancing along the sidewalk. New York City was always busier this time of year as tourists came to do Christmas shopping or stay for the week to watch the Rockefeller Center Christmas tree be erected, then lit, in all its spectacular glory.

"Oh, my gosh, I haven't told you yet!" Miranda exclaimed, as she hung onto his arm. "Grace wants me to be a bridesmaid at her and Charles's wedding. I guess we'll be going dress shopping soon."

"I'm sure you'll enjoy that. Is there a woman alive who doesn't like shopping?"

"Probably one or two, but I'm not one of them." She grinned up at him. "Do you have any Christmas shopping you want to do while you're still on vacation? It's still early—we have time to look in a few stores."

He looked down at her rosy cheeks and the cute knit hat she had pulled over her soft hair, and realized that Christmas shopping had been off his to-do list for so long, he hadn't even thought about it. He definitely needed to come up with something to give this special woman to show how much she'd brought to his life.

"The only Christmas shopping I need to do is for you, and since I can't do that with you peeking, the answer is no."

"You don't have to get anything for me. I'm still wearing the amazing ring I was supposed to give back to you at the end of this week."

"Except that's changed now. An engagement ring given to my beautiful bride before Christmas can't qualify as a Christmas gift, too."

The eyes lifting to his looked like maybe they were smiling and worried at the same time. "I… Don't you ever buy gifts for your parents?"

His gut tightened, not wanting to think about his parents and their disappointment in him and their nastiness to Miranda. Glad to be far away from that disaster. "Not unless I'm there with them at Christmas, which hasn't happened in a long time. They don't expect me to ship anything from here."

"Do they send you gifts?"

"Usually a basket of fruits and candies that I take to the hospital for the nursing staff or share with other medics. I've told them not to bother, but I guess parents never stop thinking about what their offspring are eating. Or they feel required to make the gesture." He looked down at her again, wondering why she was frowning. "Why?"

"Because I can't help but feel bothered by this…situation. I mean, we're engaged for real now, but you don't seem to want them involved in any way. You haven't called once since we've been back. And now you tell me you don't bother with Christmas gifts. I'm betting not even a card."

"All true. And your point?"

"It's not good. I mean, for better or worse, they're your parents and they love you. I know deep inside you love them too. You can't just shut them out."

"Watch me." He shoved down the uneasy feeling in his chest, the tiny nagging voice that told him Miranda was right. That he shouldn't completely shut out the two people who'd given him life, especially now, when their lives had become so difficult. But both had made unreasonable demands on him. Refused to accept beautiful and special Miranda as his future wife, and if he had to choose her over his parents, he absolutely would.

Miranda opened her mouth then shut it again, obviously deciding not to pursue it. Which he was more than happy about. Talking wasn't going to change a thing, other than to make his stomach hurt and make Miranda worry about it.

He'd made his decision about his future, and was more than happy with that.

"Come in here." Miranda took an abrupt left toward a shop doorway, dragging Mateo with her.

He looked around and saw they'd entered a jewelry store. "You have some jewelry you'd like to show me that I can choose from for you for Christmas? A bit of a surprise, but not completely a surprise?" He dropped a kiss to her temple, let it linger there. "I like that idea."

"Not for me. For your mother."

"My mother?" What was she talking about? "First, I haven't given my mother jewelry since I bought her some gaudy fake gold and diamond pin when I was about nine years old. And didn't I just tell you I don't buy her gifts at all? Especially now, considering how upset she is with me."

"All the more reason to buy her something, as a peace offering. A…a really nice bracelet that she could wear and think of you every time she does."

"Miranda." He held her face in his hands, trying to understand why she was so concerned about his relationship with his parents when he wasn't. After all, he'd been more or less estranged from them for years, and this was nothing new. "You need to stop worrying about this. I don't think she needs or wants anything to remind her of me. Especially when every time she thinks of me she concentrates on all the ways I disappoint them. Let's forget all that and enjoy our last night together before work gets hectic again, hmm?"

He read the hesitation in her eyes, then sighed in relief when she finally smiled and took his hand. "All right. I have to be at the hospital early, so what should we do that won't keep us out late? Enjoy a sweet dessert somewhere?"

"There's one thing I can think of that I'd like to do that won't keep us out late but might keep us up late, and would taste very, very sweet," he said in her ear, glad to be moving to a conversation that involved being alone and kissing and making love. "How about we go to my apartment, and I'll show you what I have?"

"I can't imagine what that would be," she said in faux, wide-eyed innocence. "Did you bake a cake? Buy ice cream?"

He had to laugh, tugging her close and dropping a kiss on her luscious mouth. How had he gotten so lucky as to have the fates throw him and Miranda together in such a surprising way? To meet a woman who was smart and sweet and fun as well, making him feel things, want things he'd never known were missing from his life?

"I think you already know what my very favorite sweet dessert is, and I can't wait to enjoy it all night long."

* * *

Miranda grabbed her phone to silence the alarm so as to not awaken the man whose warm, masculine and delicious-feeling body was half-draped over hers. Very gently, she moved his heavy arm from her waist and twisted to look at him. At his chiseled jaw and sensually shaped mouth that had kissed every inch of her body last night. At the dark lashes fanning his cheeks, looking almost boyish in a relaxed sleep. Far different from the fire and passion he'd shown her throughout the night as they'd made love in a way she'd never dreamed possible. In a way that had scorched her body at the same time it reached deeply and tenderly all the way inside her soul.

It was beyond wonderful at the same time it felt awful. She just couldn't feel truly good about it. Good in a way that told her without a doubt that she was doing the right thing by holding him close and marrying him. Distancing him, both physically and emotionally, from his family. Without their engagement, he might well have stayed in Spain longer. Probably would have. He'd have been there for his father, and maybe even have had honest conversations with his mother that would have brought them closer.

All of them were still grieving Emilio's death, and she knew well that people didn't always think rationally during times of extreme stress and pain and worry. Nearly going off the deep end after her mother had died had shown her that first-hand, but at the time she hadn't even realized she couldn't think straight for a long time.

She reached to tenderly stroke her fingertip across his strong cheekbone, and a sad smile touched her lips as his face twitched in response. Marrying him after such a short time, in the midst of a true-life crisis for him and for his parents, would be wrong. She'd been responsible for ripping a hole in the fabric of the Davenports' lives thirteen years ago, and couldn't allow herself to do that to another family.

Stepping away was the only fair and right thing to do, no matter how much she loved him. Losing his brother and facing responsibilities he wasn't sure he wanted meant that Mateo wasn't in a good place emotionally to make a big, life-changing decision.

No, she had to let Mateo think longer about what he should do. Allowing his family to work together to heal wouldn't happen if she was permanently bound to the man. He'd been so convinced for so long that he never wanted to get married, it seemed impossible that he'd completely changed his mind in one week, much as she'd wanted to believe he could.

If it was meant to be, perhaps someday in the future they'd be together again. But for now, leaving him to figure out what he really wanted, when grief and anger and feelings of inadequacy were clouding his judgement, was her only choice. To know for certain if he really loved her, or if being with her had simply been temporary pain relief.

A lump formed in her throat as she oh-so-gently touched her lips to his forehead. Why did love have to hurt so much? The effort it took to somehow force herself to slip from the bed felt nearly impossible. To dress for work and leave a note for Mateo, explaining why it had to be over between them, at least for now, hoping he'd understand. Hoping he'd be able to look inside his heart and mind more clearly with her gone.

Clicking the door quietly behind her, she crept away with dawn rising between the tall buildings of New York City. The wind that bit her skin and whipped her hair felt colder than it had yesterday. Her chest felt like someone had kicked all the air out of it, knowing that Mateo's arm wouldn't be holding her close, to make her feel safe, to make her feel appreciated, to make her feel loved.

Head down against the wind fighting her progress, she made herself keep going. Hoping that letting him go would truly help him find his way.

CHAPTER TWELVE

FOR AT LEAST the tenth time, Mateo read the note Miranda had left him, and it didn't make any more sense now than it had the first time he'd read it.

Miranda was the most giving, loving, astute woman he'd ever met. A woman anyone could rely on to be honest and trustworthy. A woman who would always be there to help anyone who needed it.

Which meant this staggering news, her breaking off their engagement, breaking off any kind of relationship with him, was clearly all his fault, not hers.

And yet he couldn't figure out how she could be so sure that he only thought he loved her because of the stress he'd been under. That it was all a reaction to his brother dying, to his life changing in ways he wasn't comfortable with. That she was a passing thing to him.

Hadn't he shown her in so many ways how

much he loved her? Couldn't she see it in his eyes, feel it in his touch, sense it when they made love?

He crumpled the note in his hand and set it next to the ring she'd left on the table. Yeah, maybe he did have to deal with his grief and guilt, his parents' pain and the situation back home before he could begin to think about another big life change. But they could have stayed together, without setting a date for a wedding yet, right? Spent time learning about one another, loving one another?

But instead she was gone. And he was left trying to cope with the ache in his chest she'd left behind.

He dragged his hand through his hair, forcing himself to face the truth. His insistence that they make their engagement real had come too fast. He saw that now. He'd exposed her to the stress and upheaval back at home and given her a glimpse of the same upheaval he felt in his heart and mind and gut. So, of course, she couldn't believe he really loved her. Wanted her in his life forever. Hadn't he spent half their time together telling her why he never wanted to get married?

Damn it.

He wanted to run after her, somehow convince her that his love for her was real, and not a reaction to everything else going on in his life.

But maybe the truth was that Miranda deserved better than him, which he'd thought all along. A man who had the kind of stable family life she craved, that she wanted for herself, that she'd never fully had. God knew, he wasn't that man, the way he'd let his brother down. With his relationship with his parents a complete wreck.

Maybe his attitude about his parents, his avoiding the grief and guilt he felt from Emilio being gone, really was selfish. Maybe he'd been being selfish with Miranda, too.

Not going after her to try to convince her they should be together made his heart feel like a huge hunk of it was being chopped off. She made him feel whole in a way he'd never felt in his life. But would that be what was best for her?

It was time to face the hard truth that it damn well wasn't.

Hadn't she been learning to be the kind of person she wanted to be? A person who knew her self-worth wasn't tied to her past or her relationship with Vanessa Davenport? She was teaching him that he needed to fix himself first, just like she was doing.

He couldn't give her damaged goods, which was what he was right now. He had to let her go.

He sat quietly, his heart aching as he absorbed the pain of that reality. He'd thought having to live at the Castillo de Adelaide Fernanda would have changed his life in a bad way. After having Miranda in his life for just the briefest time, he knew with certainty his life really had completely changed. Without her in it, he'd have a hole in his world that only she could fill.

The end of a twelve-hour shift always left Miranda exhausted, but today she felt more jittery than tired. All week she'd worked extra hours, trying to keep busy so she had less time to think about Mateo. To wonder what he was doing. If he'd talked with his parents. If he'd thought more about her suggestion to go back home for a while to think things through.

If he missed her as much as she missed him.

Every time an ambulance brought a patient to the ER, she found herself looking to see who the EMT was. Not once all week had it been Mateo, and she'd cautiously hoped he might have gone to Spain. But when she casually asked one of his co-workers, she was shocked to learn he'd asked to be moved to a different precinct.

Guilt clawed at her chest. He hadn't gone home. Her breaking up with him had just pushed him to move on to a different job. He'd talked about how much he enjoyed working as a team with the other EMTs, and now he had to learn to work with new people all over again.

Miranda grabbed her coat from her locker and

slowly headed to the hospital's back door, wondering if she'd made a mistake. Had she abandoned him right when he'd needed her most? Should she have stayed to be there for him, gently encouraging him to talk with his parents? Nudging him to go home again to try to mend the fences that had yawned even wider apart after she'd agreed to fake an engagement?

Feeling too unsettled to think about going to her apartment, she decided she should stop being such a hermit and mingle with the New Yorkers and visitors who were enjoying the Rockefeller Center Christmas tree that had gone up the day before. It would remind her of skating with Mateo on the plaza, but it wasn't as though he wasn't on her mind anyway.

Maybe one good thing could come of this pain and emptiness she felt. Maybe she'd change the way she lived in New York, get out and explore and have adventures like Mateo had encouraged her to. Be bolder and braver. Or would that just make her miss him even more, wishing so much he was there to share it all with her?

Standing in front of the huge pine tree, she hardly noticed the cold wind stinging her cheeks. Dozens of people were there, but somehow she felt more alone than she could remember ever feeling in her life. She took a breath, forcing herself to participate in the cheers as thousands of colorful lights came on and brightened all of Rockefeller Center.

Couples and families stood smiling, holding hands and hugging, and Miranda swallowed back the tears that threatened to spill over. Wishing so much that Mateo was standing there with her, holding her hand, smiling at her. That his mother, who loved Christmas and holiday decorations, could be there too, bringing Ana some happiness in the midst of such a difficult time in her life.

As she stared at the sparkling tree, bringing happiness to so many people, an idea seeped into Miranda's mind, then grew.

She'd been the one to bring chaos and stress to the Davenports' home thirteen years ago. Had made things worse between Mateo and his parents, widening the divide between them. What if it was time for her to be the one to fix things instead? To mend a rift and bring people closer together instead of pulling them apart?

A small smile started to form, banishing her tears. Optimism slowly filled her heart, followed by a conviction that it was the absolute right thing to do. Christmas was about miracles, wasn't it? Maybe, just maybe, she could make a miracle of her own.

Mateo trudged up the stairs to his apartment, wondering when the days might start feeling different from one another. When Saturdays and Mondays and Thursdays wouldn't all blur together into a week of just going through the motions. Taking care of patients, then running errands, then heading back to his apartment, alone. Seeing happy couples hand in hand and kissing, which made him physically ache. Seeing mothers and fathers and children laughing and window-shopping and obviously enjoying the kind of close family bond only parents and siblings were blessed to have.

How had his family gotten it so wrong? How much of it was his fault? The more he thought about what Miranda had said in her note, the more he wondered if he'd blamed his parents when, truthfully, they'd all had a hand in the way their family had fractured over the years.

He'd been more than happy to stay extra time in the army when Emilio had been released early. He was the one who'd left the country and rarely returned for visits. For the first time, he tried to see it from his parents' perspective, and he could understand why they'd been angry—hurt, really—at the distance he'd put between them, both physically and emotionally.

He fingered the box in his pocket that he'd planned to mail home, and suddenly realized that wasn't good enough. That Miranda, as usual, had been right. That he needed to go to Spain and deliver it himself. He had to quit hiding from the guilt and pain about Emilio. Now that Miranda was gone from his life, protecting himself from that pain by living in New York wasn't working anymore.

He'd go home and spend time with his parents. Really spend time with them, and let them know that, despite being gone for so many years, he loved them. Talk about how much he'd loved Emilio, confess the guilt he felt over not being there for him during tough times. Deal with that pain. And once he had, once his family was more together than it was now, he'd come back and find Miranda. Maybe if he had his life together, she'd finally see that he truly loved her.

Yeah, that's what had to happen, and the sooner it happened, the sooner he could come back and see Miranda again. He hurried to his apartment to make a plane reservation to Spain, pronto. He unlocked his door then came to a dead stop. Stunned, because there were three people sitting in his living room.

The three people who meant the most in the world to him.

"Hello, Mateo," Miranda said, her voice sounding a little thin as she stood. "I thought you should have an early Christmas gift. A visit from your parents, so you can talk things through."

"Miranda. Madre. Padre. I can't...believe you're all here."

His mother stood and walked to him, her face anxious and strained and full of something else. Remorse?

"Mateo, I'm so sorry we have been such fools, only expressing anger and disappointment instead of telling you how much we love you."

To his shock, her eyes filled with tears, and he closed the gap between them to take her hands. "Mother, it's all right. I've made mistakes too. Things have been hard for all of us."

"Miranda tells me that you believe we loved Emilio more. That's just not true." She squeezed his hands tightly. "We loved you every bit as much, and were heartbroken when you left."

"I didn't think you needed me there, with Emilio taking care of everything."

"We always needed you, if only to have you close." A tremulous smile touched her lips. "Emilio missed you, too, and I understand now how you tried to protect him. The two of you always had such a special bond, and I know you were a good brother to him."

His throat closed, knowing that wasn't true. And now was the time to confess that. "I let him down. I should have been there for him when things with Camilla got worse. I might have kept him from paragliding that day."

"No." His mother shook her head sadly. "It wasn't your job to ensure that Emilio made good decisions. If anyone must feel guilt, it's your father and me for insisting they marry. For being so blind."

That statement struck Mateo like a hard blow. He realized they all shared the same pain, feelings of guilt they had to let go of to move on.

Mateo's gaze moved to Miranda. Their eyes met, and just seeing that beautiful blue from across the room made his chest ache. Made him want to grab her into his arms and never let her go, no matter if she tried to leave him again or not.

And wouldn't that make him the same, pushy man he'd been last time?

No, what he needed to do was romance her, give her the time he hadn't given her before. Prove to her how much he loved her. How much he needed her. How much he wanted the forever-after with her he'd never thought he'd want with anyone.

"I need to talk to you, Miranda."

"Talking with your parents is more important." She looked down, then away, apparently wanting to look anywhere but at him, which scared the hell out of him. But he had to force himself to breathe and be patient. "I think they have other things they want to say."

"Yes, we do," his mother said.

It was all he could do to turn his attention from the woman he loved to focus on his mother as she continued. "We're very sorry for trying to make you move back home. We'll stop trying to make you step into Emilio's shoes, if only you'll do what you already promised. Which I don't think you'll mind, *sí*? That you'll come visit sometimes, and bring Miranda with you. That's all we want."

"Bring Miranda with me?" His heart thumped in his chest as he swung his attention back to her, wondering if for some reason she'd told them they were still engaged. Then again, he hadn't told them they weren't, so who knew what they thought? "I would love to do that, but Miranda broke off our engagement, even though I'm crazy in love with her."

"What?" His mother swung toward Miranda, her eyes wide. "You didn't tell me this! How could you leave my Mateo? He is the best man you could possibly want."

That his mother was saying those words about him were unbelievable enough, and her next words astonished him even more.

"You must convince Miranda to marry you, Mateo," she said in the commanding voice he was used to. Hearing it this time would have made him smile if the stakes weren't so high.

"She is wonderful, coming to us and insisting we all get past our frustrations with one another. Talk about Emilio and how much we miss him. If you come to Spain for an extended visit, she could even take over the old doctor's office and see patients there. Locals, and your father and I, would be most grateful not to have to always go to Barcelona to get medical advice and treatment."

"Yes. We need a doctor, and Miranda has already shown how good she is," his father chimed in.

"A very interesting idea, Madre and Padre." He reached for his mother and gave her a hug, wanting to end this particular visit fast so he could get on with the next important reconnection—with his ex-fiancée. "I have to talk with Miranda about all that, but first I do have a gift for you."

"A gift?"

The surprise on his mother's face would have made him feel guilty enough, but when tears swam in her eyes again he thrashed himself for neglecting her for so long. But those days were over.

"Miranda's suggestion. I hope you like it."

He held out the wrapped box, and his mother opened it, then gasped as the tears overflowed. "A bracelet, to go with the one Emilio gave me."

She lifted her watery gaze to his. "Does this mean you're coming home for good?"

He glanced at Miranda, and his heart stumbled because, instead of looking like she wanted to run into his arms, she was biting her lip and looking worried, the same way she had before she'd left him. "That has a lot to do with Miranda. Will you leave us alone to talk about it? I'll come to your hotel for breakfast to work out some details."

"Fine. Good." She gave his father the "look", which meant she wanted to give them the privacy he'd asked for. "Here's our hotel information. Let us know what time. Come, Rafael."

Mateo hugged them both, and already the heavy weight that had hung on his shoulders the past six months felt lighter. Except there was another, even bigger weight crushing his chest until he could barely breathe.

Closing the door behind them, he moved toward Miranda, not sure whether he should fold her in his arms and kiss her, or give her space, which he hadn't done enough of before. He pulled in a breath and forged forward with the most critical conversation he'd had in his life.

"Thank you for reaching out to them and bringing them here. You're incredible. The most special woman I've ever known. And now my parents finally realize it, too."

* * *

Miranda's heart stuttered at his words before she reminded herself that him saying she was a special woman wasn't a big deal, under the circumstances. "Your situation helped me see things about my own life I hadn't fully realized. That I'd carried the weight of Vanessa's dislike for all these years to the point where I'd let it dictate who I believed I was. That I was the cause of the rift in my family. But I know now that I can't change that situation, that all I have control over is how I react to it. It struck me that you were doing the same thing, and I felt bad about making your family situation worse. So I brought them here to help you all put that baggage behind you. Move toward a better relationship that will make you all happy."

"Miranda." He wrapped his arms around her, bringing her close to the warm body she'd missed so much. "It's terrible that you've believed your family issues were your fault when in truth the problems were caused by your father."

"Hey, I'm not the only one. You were sure your parents thought Emilio was better than you, and you believed it, too. But of course it's not true at all."

"Maybe the reason we fell in love so fast is because we're more alike than we knew. That we were meant to help each other let go of those things. To have wonderful adventures together, bring out the best in each other."

"I don't think you really love me, Mateo," she whispered, wanting so much to be wrong. "It was just the difficulties in your life that made you believe you did."

"Is that why I think about you all day, every day? Why I close my eyes and remember how you looked with the breeze blowing your hair on the funicular? Why I remember how tough you were in the tunnel, and all the ways you're a great doctor? Why I can taste you and feel your soft skin against mine even when I'm sleeping? Why I've been completely miserable without you for the past week? I guess you're right. I guess that's not love."

Her chest expanded with emotion, but she was so afraid to believe it. So afraid he'd regret marrying when he'd never wanted that in his life. She looked up at him, tears stinging the backs of her eyes. "I don't know what to say. What to think."

"Up at Montserrat, you told me you'd had a miracle in your life once, and I said I didn't believe in miracles. But I was wrong." He cupped her face in his hands, and the tender look in his eyes stopped her breath. "You made me believe in miracles, Miranda, and my miracle is you. You've made me see how I shut myself off from being hurt. By my parents, by the guilt I felt over not being there for my brother, by any woman after seeing how much he was hurt by his wife. You've done that, too. Not believed in yourself enough. What do you say we spend our lives believing in each other? Loving each other? Please say yes."

"Yes." She flung her arms around his neck and sniffed back the tears. "I love you so much. I've missed you so much."

He lowered his mouth and kissed her, long and sweet and wonderful. When he pulled back, she felt dazed, even as a happiness bloomed in her chest unlike anything she'd experienced in her life. Then she frowned when his warm body moved away from hers and he went to his bedroom.

"Um, am I supposed to follow you in there?"

"Not quite yet. Soon." He emerged again, smiling, his eyes dark and alive, looking at her with such clear, real love she felt weak all over again. "First, this. Will you marry me, Dr. Davenport? For real, and forever?"

She looked down at the beautiful blue stone winking at her, and held out her hand. "Yes, Mr. Mateo. For real and forever and as soon as possible."

He laughed, sliding the ring on her finger before kissing her senseless.

"So," he said as they came up for breath, "how do you feel about moving to Spain? You can become the region's doctor. But only if you like the idea. We can stay here, and just go a few times a year if you prefer. I'll be happy any place in the world, so long as you're there with me."

"I fell in love with your home almost as fast as I fell in love with you." It was true, and the idea of living in that beautiful place made her chest nearly overflow with the joy of all he was offering her. "Miranda Alves, wife of the future Duke of Pinero, has a nice sound to it, don't you think?"

"Yes." He kissed her again before pressing his forehead to hers. "Almost as wonderful a sound as both of us saying 'I do'."

* * * * *

Welcome to the
CHRISTMAS IN MANHATTAN
six-book series

Available now:

SLEIGH RIDE WITH THE SINGLE DAD
by Alison Roberts
A FIREFIGHTER IN HER STOCKING
by Janice Lynn
THE SPANISH DUKE'S HOLIDAY PROPOSAL
by Robin Gianna
THE RESCUE DOC'S CHRISTMAS MIRACLE
by Amalie Berlin

Coming soon:

CHRISTMAS WITH THE BEST MAN
by Susan Carlisle
NAVY DOC ON HER CHRISTMAS LIST
by Amy Ruttan